Ella felt them draw together, his palm gently caressing her cheek, her hands on his shoulders as she gazed up at him. And then their lips found each other, and they were joined in the sweetest, deepest kiss. Ella's body tingled. No kiss had ever felt this way before. Down in the valley, the church bells were ringing out.

"Oh, no!" The church bells were ringing midnight! Ella pulled back suddenly. *I can't leave now.* Ella longed to stay with this boy with all her heart and soul.

"This has been the best night of my life!" she told him. "But I have to go."

"Wait, please!" he called after her. "I don't even know your name."

But Ella had already reached the edge of the parking lot and was running toward the little blue sports car. She moved faster and felt one glass slipper fly off her foot. But there was no time to stop and pick it up.

The party was over. The dream had vanished. And Ella had a long, cold ride home. But the wonder of the evening was enough to make her feel warm. It had been as mysterious and magical as falling in love. Yes, falling in love—if only for one perfect night.

Look for more books in the romantic series
Once Upon a Dream:

The Rose: A Novel Based on Beauty and the Beast

Once Upon a Dream

At Midnight

A Novel
Based on *Cinderella*

Jennifer Baker

SCHOLASTIC INC.
New York   Toronto   London   Auckland   Sydney

No part of this publication may be reproduced in whole or in part, or stored in a retrieval system, or transmitted in any form or by any means, electronic, mechanical, photocopying, recording, or otherwise, without written permission of the publisher. For information regarding permission, write to Scholastic Inc., 555 Broadway, New York, NY 10012.

ISBN 0-590-25947-4

Produced by Daniel Weiss Associates, Inc.
33 West 17th Street, New York, NY 10011

12 11 10 9 8 7 6 5 4 3 2 1   5 6 7 8 9/9 0/0

Printed in the U.S.A.   01

First Scholastic printing, September 1995

One

Ella Browning had butterflies in her stomach. She listened as the first notes of the wedding march filled the sweet, mild fall air. *Here comes the bride!* announced the vibrating strings of the stately quartet set up on her lawn. The familiar tune made her almost as nervous as if *she* were the one getting married, not her father.

Standing at her father's side, Ella felt jittery as she looked out at the rows of guests. At the sound of the wedding march, the crowd swiveled around in their folding chairs to eye the sliding glass doors to the house, watching for the bride to emerge.

Ella glanced up at her father and smiled. He was so handsome in his simple tux, a tiny white rose in his lapel. His salt-and-pepper hair was thick and wavy, his dark eyes gleaming. But he seemed nervous, too, fidgeting with the bow tie Ella had knotted for him.

It was all happening so suddenly. Her father had started dating Lucinda only a few months earlier, and Ella had met her and her two daughters for the first time only a couple of weeks ago. Ella wished she'd felt better about that first meeting. It had been so strange to see a woman she didn't even know, draped all over her father like a second skin.

"And in front of half the town!" Ella had recounted to her best friend, Steph, the next day in school. "Lucinda was kissing and touching Dad right in the middle of surf and turf at the Plow and Anchor. Her daughters were too busy fighting over clothes they'd borrowed from each other to even notice, but Lucinda seemed determined to make Dad think they were alone. It was like I didn't even exist."

"Major public display of affection, huh?" Steph had commented. "We should be that lucky when we're their age. Actually, we should be that lucky now."

Remembering Steph's comment, Ella laughed to herself. It made her feel a bit calmer. Okay, maybe Dad *was* lucky. He certainly seemed to think so. And he'd assured Ella he knew what he was doing. "Now you'll have a mother again—sisters, a real family," he'd told Ella as she'd helped him get dressed in his wedding suit that morning. "And we'll have a good life with Lucinda. She appreciates the finer things—really knows how to get what she wants."

He did have a point there. The grounds had never looked more beautiful, Ella thought. The high hedges that marked the property boundaries were freshly trimmed, the small, round tables placed on the wide lawn were set with only the finest linen, crystal, and silver. In the middle of each table was a vase of roses in full bloom, white, red, and every shade of pink in between. The grass looked greener than usual, somehow. And the sky seemed bluer, with a few light, wispy clouds. It was as if Lucinda had Mother Nature under her thumb, along with Dad.

Ella took her father's hand and gave it a squeeze. He kissed her on the cheek, and then, as the music swelled, they both looked toward the house. The glass doors slid open and Lucinda stepped out, accompanied by her daughters, Staci and Drew, on either side of her. She wore a white strapless silk gown that followed her curves to about the knee, then flared gently to the floor. Her jet-black hair was gathered in a loose knot at her long, slender neck. Her dark eyes and bright red lips stood out against her milk pale skin. A slender diamond choker shimmered at her throat.

Staci and Drew wore similarly cut dresses—Staci's pale pink and Drew's peach—though neither dress hung quite the way it did on their mother. Drew, the younger daughter, seemed to have inherited all of Lucinda's curves but none of her slenderness, and Staci had all the slenderness and none of the curves. But they both made up for it by being perfectly dressed and made up.

Ella had watched as she'd gotten dressed with them in her room earlier that day. She couldn't believe how long they'd taken to carefully style every last lock of their hair, how critically they'd surveyed each other's faces.

"That shadow's much too dark."

"You need more eyeliner."

"You really ought to get your bangs trimmed . . ."

Ella swept her hand down her long brown hair, as if to smooth it out. She was feeling a bit self-conscious now, thinking about Lucinda and her perfectly dressed daughters. Ella hoped her lipstick wasn't smudged.

Ella's father squeezed her hand, snapping her out of her thoughts. She watched Lucinda glide down the grassy aisle in her spike-heeled satin shoes. Elegant. Assured. Ella couldn't imagine being so cool on such an important occasion. In those heels, she'd probably trip over the hem of such a long dress.

For a moment, Ella pictured herself where Lucinda was now, imagined herself as the bride—excited, scared, happy. She could almost feel the flush in her cheeks, the crowd's eyes all riveted on her. She'd be wearing her mother's antique lace wedding dress with the full skirt, a garland of flowers around her head.

Who would be her groom, standing where her father was now? Who would be waiting to take her arm and declare his eternal love? Ella knew he'd be kind and funny and smart. He'd be handsome—oh, so handsome. But Ella couldn't put a face to her daydream. She'd dated a few guys at school, but she hadn't found the right one. Not yet.

Her daydream broke apart as Lucinda and her daughters drew near. Ella felt her father withdraw his hand from hers. Ella stepped to the side, as she'd done in rehearsal the evening before. Staci and Drew stepped to the other side of the wedding altar. And her father and Lucinda took their places before the dark-suited, bespectacled judge.

"Welcome," the judge began in a rich, deep voice. "We are gathered on this joyous occasion, to bring together in holy matrimony . . ."

This is the real thing. This was no daydream. Dad was getting married. Lucinda was about to become Mrs. Browning.

Ella felt a pinch of sadness at that last thought. Mrs. Browning. Once upon a time, that had been Mom.

"No one will ever replace your mother," Dad had said to Ella when he'd announced his engagement. "I'll never forget her, never stop loving her. But it's time to leave the sorrow behind."

And it was true. There had been too many long, lonely years for Dad. And recently, Ella had begun to notice how tired he looked around the eyes. But now, as the judge spoke of love and commitment, Dad was smiling. He looked young again. Despite her misgivings about Lucinda, as long as her father was happy, Ella was happy for him.

"Do you, Kenneth, take Lucinda to be your lawfully wedded wife?" the judge asked. "To love and to cherish, for better, for worse, in sickness and in health, forsaking all others as long as you both shall live?"

Ella's father smiled at his bride. "I do."

"Do you, Lucinda, take Kenneth to be your lawfully wedded husband? To love and to cherish, for better, for worse, in sickness and in health, forsaking all others as long as you both shall live?"

Lucinda gave Ella's father a perfect hundred-watt smile, then beamed her brightness out at their guests. "I do."

The judge turned to Ella. "The ring?"

Ella slipped the heavy, smooth gold band from her pocket and held it out.

"Kenneth," said the judge, "I want you to take the ring from your daughter and place it on Lucinda's finger."

Ella watched her father slip the ring on Lucinda's left ring finger. Then Lucinda took a larger wedding band from Staci, and put it on Ella's father's hand. This was it.

"I now pronounce you husband and wife."

Ella felt a strange tug of emotions as her father leaned down and gave Lucinda a long, romantic kiss. Then she joined in the applause.

Dad finally pulled back and let Lucinda go. He turned to Ella, wrapping her in a hug. "We did it, Princess!" he whispered. He sounded so happy.

"Congratulations, Dad," Ella said genuinely.

"And now my new daughters," her dad said, moving toward Staci and Drew.

Ella looked over at Lucinda and held her arms out awkwardly. Lucinda took a step toward her. She brought her perfectly lipsticked lips to within a few inches of the side of Ella's face—and kissed the air.

Staci and Drew, pulling themselves from Ella's father's hug, tossed Ella stiff smiles.

Staci and Drew are my sisters now, Ella thought, biting her lip. *But I feel like a stranger to them.* Well, they'd only met a few times before. Lucinda and her daughters were sure to warm up when they all got to know each other better.

"One big, happy family," Ella's father cheered. "My happy family."

Ella prayed he was right.

William de Montroig Frederic Henri Windmere Villacampo—Prince Will—pulled off a muddy lacrosse shoe and tossed it at the foot of his locker. Prince Will preferred polo. Lacrosse seemed like a joke to him. Sure, you ran after the ball with a stick. But it was as if someone had let the horses run loose, and the players had to stumble around on their own. Still, Will was Chason's best player, and besides, playing lacrosse instead of polo was a small price to pay for being far away from home.

Will's teammates tramped mud in from the playing field after the first practice of the season. Their voices echoed off the metal lockers.

"Hey, Will! Nice pass to Jameson," said his

buddy Chris, snapping a rolled-up towel at Will's thigh.

"Thanks." *It's so great to be one of the guys again,* Will thought. *No more royal protocol.*

"So—I haven't had a chance to find out how your summer was." Chris sat down on the bench next to Will and ran a hand through his damp blond curls. "Parties? Important people? Pretty ladies?"

Will laughed. "Yes, yes, and yes." He knew it sounded like a dream come true. But it was hard work, too—smiling brightly for the public each and every night, saying the right things, behaving just as the crown prince was supposed to, always feeling the weight of centuries of traditions and rules. But Will knew he couldn't explain that to his friend. Chris would never understand.

"Who was the most famous person you met? The most beautiful girl?" Chris pressed, thirsty for details.

"Did I hear someone say beautiful girls?" Will heard the note of longing in their friend Kenny's voice a moment before he appeared, wet from the shower, with a towel around his tubby waist.

"Yeah, Will here was just telling me all about the privileges of his royal summer," Chris said, with a sigh of envy.

"You mean things like being the honored guest at a dinner for the Society for the Re-creation of Medieval Cuisine?" Will asked, shaking his head. "Have a hunk of venison and some stale bread. Man, it was all I could do to keep from excusing myself from the table and hopping the next plane to the nearest Burger Barn." Chris and Kenny laughed. "It never ceases to amaze me how many events and obligations there are in a tiny country that has fewer people than the state of Connecticut."

"Yeah, but still—you're the prince of that country. A real, live prince," Kenny said, awed.

"Yo, Kenny, I was just trying to forget about all that," Will said lightly.

"Not so fast. You don't think you're getting off without telling us about the girls," Chris demanded. "All those fancy parties must have been swarming with them."

Will shrugged. "Nothing much to tell. The palace arranged most of my dates for the events on my busy schedule. And there wasn't anyone really special." Will felt a vague pinch of longing. "You guys probably have more stories than I do."

A grin spread across Chris's handsome square-jawed face. "Well, it was a pretty good summer over here. Gorgeous girl teaching tennis with me— just finished her freshman year of college . . ."

Will arched an eyebrow. "An older woman, huh?"

"Well, yeah, but there was a younger girl I was teaching, too. Actually, there were two girls who took lessons from me—one the first month and one the second."

"Wait. And you went out with all three of them?" Kenny asked, opening his eyes wide.

"Man, that's why there aren't enough for the rest of us," Will joked.

"Yeah, right. Like every girl in this whole school—maybe the whole world—isn't absolutely dying to go out with his Royal Willness," Chris commented.

Will busied himself, peeling off his dirty uniform. He hoped Chris and Kenny didn't notice his cheeks burning with embarrassment. "Well, it's not really me they're interested in. It's my title. Like, you know—if I weren't a prince. . ."

"And you're holding out for your one true love, huh?" Chris teased. "The girl who's going to love you for your soul? The one who'd love you if you were just the guy next door?"

Kenny tugged his jeans over his large body. "Prince, pauper. It doesn't matter to me. I'd take anyone who'd love me for whatever reason. I'm not picky."

Will laughed. "So you think I'm picky? Listen, is it so awful to want to meet the right girl?"

"Not awful. Just . . . I don't know," Chris said. "I mean, the perfect girl. That's about as big a fairy tale as—"

"As being a prince in this day and age?" Will supplied. "I know it meant more back when the palace made real decisions—the kind presidents and prime ministers and politicians make now. Sometimes I think I'm just one big photo opp." Will shrugged. "But, hey, it's a job. And the benefits are pretty great," he added less seriously. "The thing is, I just think finding the right girl to share it all with might help me find some meaning in it. Know what I mean?"

Kenny nodded, but Will could see he'd lost Chris. A notorious flirt, Chris just couldn't seem to understand that sometimes one special girl was better than many random ones.

"Well, it doesn't really matter anyway," Will concluded. "My parents'll probably find a wife for me before I find her myself."

"A wife!" Chris sounded shocked. "Hold on, man. How'd we go from dating to marrying? I don't plan on even thinking about that for a long, long time."

Kenny whistled through his teeth. "Whoa,

that's serious stuff. I'm still working on getting the nerve up to ask a girl out."

Will suddenly felt the distance between himself and his friends. "There are hundreds and hundreds of years of tradition behind my royal title," he tried to explain. "Certain things are taken for granted. I'm supposed to find a bride—someone who can live up to the royal image, someone who can play her role just as I have to play mine. My parents have already started making what they call 'suitable suggestions.' It's one of the reasons I'm so glad to be back at school for a while."

Chris frowned. "You know, Will, I always thought you had it totally made. But when you put it that way—I don't know." He stood up and draped his towel around his shoulders. "I guess you'd better enjoy yourself while you can."

Will tried to keep it light. "I guess. And I'm counting on you two losers to help me, okay?"

But when Will thought about the future, he felt so different from everyone else. Different, and so alone.

Two

The sun streamed through the kitchen windows, and birds chirped in the trees outside as Ella slowly came downstairs early the next morning. Ella's father had set the breakfast table with their good dishes, the bone china with the delicate floral pattern. He'd squeezed fresh orange juice and was making his special buttermilk waffles. He hummed as he cooked.

Lucinda and her stuck-up daughters sat formally at the table. Ella had to remind herself that they weren't guests. Strange as it seemed, they were here to stay. This was their home now, too.

Ella felt them look her over as she entered the kitchen, and she wondered if she should have come down in her skirt and blouse, not the comfy old woolly pink bathrobe she was wearing. Lucinda and her girls were already carefully dressed, and an overwhelming odor of perfume mixed with the smell of the waffles.

"Morning," Ella said brightly, ignoring the awkward silence in the room. "Everyone sleep okay?"

"Good morning, Ella," Lucinda said. She smiled politely, but her tone was distant. "We slept fine, thank you."

"Good." Ella turned to her new stepsisters. "I hope your room was comfortable."

Drew, already munching on a muffin, ran a manicured hand through her light brown hair. Her nails were long and sculpted, shiny with red polish. "Sure," she said, with a little shrug. "Room's fine. Just needs some fixing up, right, Stace?"

"Easy for you to say," Staci said harshly. "*You've* already taken over three-quarters of the closet."

"And *you* nabbed the bed by the window," Drew shot back.

"Well, I'm older," Staci said. "If we had separate rooms, I'd have the bigger one."

"But we *don't* have separate rooms anymore," Drew said.

"Not in this place," Staci added.

Ella felt a stab of discomfort. It was as if somehow it were her fault—hers and her father's—that Drew and Staci were fighting.

"Girls," Lucinda said without much conviction.

So often during the years when it had just been Ella and her father, she had longed for a brother or sister—someone she could laugh with at the table, someone with whom she could stay up late, trading secrets long after they were supposed to be asleep, and then later, someone she could double-date with, someone whose closet she could raid, someone who understood her better than anyone else. . . . Someone who she would love even more than a best friend. The nasty coldness that passed between Drew and Staci was not even close to what she'd imagined being someone's sister would be like.

Ella took a seat at the table—not her usual one, because Drew was already sitting there. "You know, the attic's pretty nice. Big, lots of light. We could clean it out and turn it into another bedroom," Ella suggested.

"The attic?" Staci said distastefully. She shot a look at Drew. Drew wrinkled her nose. Well, at least the sisters were in agreement now.

Ella held back a sigh.

If her father noticed the tension that reigned in

the kitchen, he didn't let on. He set a plate of steaming hot waffles on the table. "Dig in," he said cheerfully. "Syrup and other fixings coming right up." He leaned down and gave Ella a kiss on the forehead. "How's my princess this morning?"

"Fine, Daddy." Ella smiled.

"And my two new princesses?" he asked, touching both Drew and Staci on their shoulders.

Staci gave a frigid smile. Drew just dug into the waffles and said nothing.

Her father was trying so hard to make this mismatched group a family.

Ella felt a stab of anger. *Drew and Staci really do think they're princesses.* Letting her father wait on them hand and foot, complaining about how their room needed fixing up, making Ella feel that *she* needed fixing up, too.

Hold on a second, Ella told herself. It had to be strange for Staci and Drew to find themselves in a new house, to be suddenly uprooted in the space of an "I do." Ella was home. In her own house, her own room. She had to remember that, and to try to be more generous until everyone grew more comfortable with the new arrangements and each other.

And besides, Dad looks so happy, Ella thought as she watched him busily serve breakfast. Her dad smiled broadly as he loaded up a tray with warm maple syrup, fresh whipped cream, and a bowl of tiny, deep red strawberries. Ella smiled back at him as he brought the tray to the table.

"Sweets for my sw—" He suddenly broke off mid-sentence, the tray dropping from his hands and crashing to the floor. The smile slipped off his lips.

"Dad!" Ella shouted.

His normally ruddy complexion went whiter than Lucinda's. He clutched his left breast, panting as if he couldn't catch his breath. Ella saw him stagger. Then he went down, too, falling in a puddle of broken dishes, blood red fruit, and sticky syrup that was spreading out on the kitchen tiles.

"Dad! Dad!" Ella rushed toward him. "Oh, no, Dad—what is it?"

Her father opened his mouth. Sweat beaded on his upper lip. His voice came out in a weak croak. "My arm, my neck. Ohhh . . ." His right hand moved to his neck, and Ella noticed with horror that his fingertips were turning blue.

She was vaguely aware of Lucinda at her side. "Kenneth? Kenneth, no!"

"Call for help!" Ella cried out. "Drew, Staci— get an ambulance!" She knelt down, barely feeling the sharp edge of a china shard as it cut into her leg. Her father's eyes were closing. "Dad. Hold on!" She grabbed his hand. "Please—help will be here soon!"

"Ella . . ." her father whispered.

"Dad!" She pressed her fingers to the inside of his wrist, not even sure what she was feeling for. Her father didn't move. There was no pulse of life under her fingers. But her own blood raced wildly. Her hands trembled. She put her ear to her father's mouth. She heard nothing, felt no soft breath on her face. "Oh, hurry! Someone, please help! Oh, hold on, Dad. Just a little while longer . . ."

Ella heard Lucinda's voice rising up into the room. "Kenneth! You can't do this to me. You promised to take care of me. You said you'd be here for me. You can't. You will not do this!"

But by the time the ambulance came squealing up the driveway, sirens wailing, it was too late.

Ella didn't think she had any more tears to cry. Her eyes were dry and stinging. Her throat was sore. The past few days were a blurry nightmare—too awful to be real. Her father, deathly pale and immobile on the kitchen floor. The emergency medic pumping her father's chest with strong hands, finally stopping and shaking his head. Lucinda's high-pitched wail.

Ella's own silent tears. The phone calls, the arrangements. The funeral, like a dark shadow of the wedding.

Ella couldn't believe her father was really gone. She'd watched as his coffin was lowered into the earth. She'd shivered, wrapping her arms around herself, with a low moan. She'd felt the salty sting of tears on her face, and she'd wanted to throw herself into the wound in the ground, joining her father in his eternal sleep.

But now, back at home, sitting on the sofa, Ella kept half-expecting her father to walk in the door, the way he did each day after work—throwing his keys onto the table in the foyer, the metal chiming against the glass. They'd lived here so long, just the two of them, that she could feel his presence everywhere—in the frayed old armchair in the corner of the room, where he used to sit and read. In the kitchen, where the dishes from that fateful breakfast still stood in the drain. Out by the vegetable garden, where plants he'd tended all summer were giving up the ghost to fall.

Dad will never see another harvest again, Ella told herself. *Never read another mystery, cook another meal.* It didn't seem possible. She felt hollow inside. This couldn't be happening. She looked over at Lucinda, sitting at the other end of the sofa, her eyes hidden by a pair of round, oversized, very dark sunglasses. She could hear Staci bossing Drew around upstairs, and she was almost glad for the sound of voices.

"I can't imagine how much more awful it would be if I were here all alone," Ella said softly to Lucinda. "It's so horrible that your wedding ended this way. . . ."

Lucinda put a hand to her glasses and pushed them up on top of her head. "Yes, it's going to be terribly hard on me," she said. She rubbed her fingers under her eyes, as if to remove the barely smudged makeup on her alabaster skin. "I don't know that someone like you can really understand."

Ella was startled. "Excuse me?" What did Lucinda mean by that? "I just lost my father. I think I have some idea of what you're feeling."

Lucinda gave a tired sigh. "Your father has always been there for you."

"Well . . . yes, until now," Ella said, swallowing against the painful reminder. What was Lucinda's point?

"And you have plenty of little friends at school," Lucinda went on. "What with your pretty face, I'm sure you have no trouble at all socially. Am I right?"

Ella shrugged. Of course she had friends—especially her best friend Steph—but she didn't exactly feel up to a chat about her social life. She furrowed her brow.

"Well, you see, some of us weren't as lucky as you," Lucinda stated. "I grew up without anyone. Alone. In a home for girls nobody wanted."

"Oh," Ella said quietly. "I didn't know. I'm sorry."

"Yes, well . . . It was the girls who fit in—the girls who had everything—who made sure I stayed on the outside," Lucinda said. "'Little Orphan Annie,' they called me. They never let me forget who I was and where I came from."

Ella felt as if Lucinda were accusing *her* of being one of those girls who'd teased her. She shifted uncomfortably on the sofa.

"So you see, I had to fight to come up in the world," Lucinda said. "And I did it—all by myself. I learned about the best life has to offer. I married the most eligible boy in town. He chose me, not all those perfect girls who'd called me names. And I helped him build his business from nothing into the most profitable construction company in the state. Oh, I thought I'd made it then. Until he thanked me by leaving me with two young daughters and running off with his bookkeeper."

Lucinda seemed almost to be talking to herself now, reciting her misfortunes and tasting their bitterness. "And your father—he left me alone, too. On my own, as always."

Ella reminded herself that this was the woman to whom her father had pledged his everlasting love. Perhaps her grief just came out in a harsh way. She thought about how happy her beloved father had been since Lucinda had come into his life. The image of his smile sent an ache of loneliness through her. For him, for his memory, Ella tried to be sympathetic toward her new stepmother.

"He didn't leave you alone," Ella said. "You have Staci and Drew . . . And, well, my father wanted us to be one big family. So you have me too."

Lucinda appeared to snap out of her reverie. "Yes. So I do." She peered at Ella intently. "You know, Ella," she began in a confidential tone.

Ella leaned forward. "Yes, Lucinda?" she said gently.

"You might want to wash up before the guests start arriving to pay their condolences," her stepmother said. "You don't want tearstains all over that perfect face you're so lucky to have."

Ella was too taken aback to answer. "And while you're up," Lucinda added levelly, "why don't you uncover all the food I had delivered, and put it out on the table . . ."

Suddenly Ella felt more tears welling up—the tears she'd thought she'd already cried out. She got up and rushed out of the room. Couldn't Lucinda spare a bit of warmth? A hug, even a nice word?

Or was she behaving this way because she hurt so much too? Ella went into the downstairs bathroom and splashed cool, clear water on her face. When her sobs finally died down, she took a few deep breaths. *Well, at least I'm not alone.*

Three

As long as the house was filled with people, Ella managed to push away the worst of her fear and loneliness. *At least I have Steph,* Ella thought as Steph looped her arm through Ella's. Steph had stuck loyally by her that entire day.

Steph had helped Ella get through visits from her father's coworkers who'd stopped by to pay their last respects, kids from school, and people from town who'd brought homemade dinners and boxes of chocolates.

Friends of Lucinda's lounged in the living room, nursing glasses of wine and talking about exotic vacations, fancy redecorating jobs, and trading pieces of society gossip. Drew and some of her friends were holding court in the kitchen, gazing over fashion magazines and helping themselves to the food mourners had brought over. Staci and her crowd told secrets up in her bedroom.

"Friendly, aren't they?" Ella asked Steph with a sigh of resignation. Ella pulled Steph upstairs to hang out in her room. "I thought having sisters was going to be more like being part of a club, or something."

Steph ran a slender hand through her tight brown curls and gave a knowing kind of laugh. "If they're anything like *my* sisters, you're lucky they don't lock you up in the garage or the attic, or something." Steph was the youngest of three girls. She frowned. "But seriously, Ella, I see what you mean about them. You'd think they could spare a bit of friendliness at a time like this." She reached over and gave Ella an impulsive hug.

Ella hugged her back, fighting the tears that caught her off guard. The last warm, sincere hug she'd gotten had been from Dad, just after the "I do's." "Thanks," she said unsteadily. "I really need a hug right about now."

"No problem," Steph said matter-of-factly. "And, Ella? Don't let those two get to you, okay? You don't want hugs from either of them, anyway."

Ella laughed shakily. "I guess not."

"You know, I've never seen Drew or Staci before. Are they from around here?" Steph asked. "They go to a different school?"

"Staci finished high school last year," Ella answered. "She's taking a year off. Drew's a day student at Chason."

"Well, la-di-da," Steph said. "Maybe that's why she's so obnoxious. Hey, you think she knows the prince?"

"Haven't seen him around here yet," Ella said. "And he's probably the only person I haven't," she added, trying a little too hard for a moment of lightness.

"Too bad," Steph said. "He looks pretty cute in the pictures I've seen of him."

Ella laughed a little more easily. It felt good to be sitting on her bed, shooting the breeze with Steph—normal.

The chatter of so many voices in the living room floated upstairs, providing a welcome screen of noise against the loneliness deep inside Ella's heart.

There was a soft knock on Ella's door. A well-lined face framed by a cap of thick white hair appeared on the other side of the door.

"Oh, hi, Mrs. Montaner," Ella said. "Come in. You've met my friend Steph." Old Mrs. Montaner lived at the end of the road in a small house with a huge garden.

"Well, of course, my dear," Mrs. Montaner said with a sad shake of her head. "You know how very, very sorry I am, and if there's anything I can do, you come right down the road and ask."

Ella nodded. "Thanks, I appreciate it."

"Oh, and I left something for you down in the kitchen," Mrs. Montaner added. "I baked you a pie with strawberries and rhubarb from my garden."

"Strawberry-rhubarb pie. Oh, wow, my Dad loves—" Ella choked on her sentence as the realization hit her like a punch in the stomach. She dropped her head into her hands. Misery flooded through her.

"Ell?" Steph said quietly.

Ella felt her friend's hand on her back. She struggled to regain her composure. "Yeah," she said, finally looking up again. "What I meant was that Dad *used* to love your homemade pies, Mrs. Montaner. Thank you."

"Yes, well, you take care of yourself, my dear," the old lady replied.

"You okay?" Steph asked as soon as Mrs. Montaner had gone back downstairs.

Ella let her eyes close. When she opened them, she shook her head slowly. It was a moment more before she trusted herself to speak. "I just can't believe it, you know? One minute I'm sort of okay, not really thinking too hard about it, and then something will happen. . . . Like that thing with the pie. Or this morning, when I was trying to reach a tray up on the top shelf of one of the kitchen cabinets. There was this split second where I was about to look around for my father to see if he'd help me."

"It must be really awful." Steph bit her lip.

"Yeah," Ella murmured.

The girls sat in silence for a few minutes. "Listen, maybe we should go downstairs, be with everyone else," Steph said finally. "Maybe the company will cheer you up a little."

"Or take my mind off things, at least." Ella thought it was a good idea. For the next few hours, she let the company and the noise and the busyness in the house take hold of her, fill her, substitute for concrete thoughts or deep feelings. And it worked . . . sort of.

But then the house began emptying out. She and Steph moved from the foyer to the living room, and Ella was caught up in a wave of good-byes.

"Call if there's anything we can do," said Mrs. Jantzen from up the road.

"I'm here if you need me, dear," said Ella's father's boss.

"You'll get through this," assured a very blond,

very tall woman who was a friend of Lucinda's.

"Thank you. Yes, I know. Good-bye. That's very kind of you. Thanks for being here with us. Bye," Ella recited almost automatically.

She knew people meant it when they offered their support. She also knew they had their own lives to live, and that when they walked out the door, they would leave Ella and her grief behind. Eventually, the neighbors would stop coming by with casseroles and flowers and kind words. The phone calls would grow fewer and farther between. Ella would be alone with the hollow ache she had been fighting down all day, feelings that she knew would sooner or later overwhelm her.

She felt the first swell of panic as the visitors trickled down to only a few. They turned up the busy chatter as if to fill the growing space in the room. No one wanted to leave too much room for grief. A few heavy drinkers finished off the wine. Some of the most thoughtful guests began clearing away plates and glasses and putting away the food. But one by one, even the last stragglers departed. Drew went upstairs to join her sister in their bedroom.

"Well, I guess I better get going," Steph finally said, as she and Ella stacked the last of the dirty coffee cups by the kitchen sink. "Will you be okay?"

Ella swallowed hard and nodded, even though it was the farthest thing from the truth. *Don't leave me here all alone,* she wanted to say. But she couldn't expect Steph to stay forever. "Let me walk you to your car," Ella said, putting off the moment she'd be alone for as long as possible.

Outside, she breathed in the first pungent breaths of fall as she watched Steph pull away down the driveway. She felt a growing sense of dread and fear. She didn't look away until Steph's car was out of sight.

Ella's legs felt impossibly heavy as she went back into the house. Her stomach was tight. She wandered into the living room, where Lucinda sat alone in the faded armchair. Ella took a seat across from her, on the sofa. She managed a sad, uncomfortable smile. Lucinda stretched her mouth in what looked more like a grimace than a returned smile.

Ella dropped her gaze to the old braided rug. The silence that chilled the room was painful. And suddenly, Ella's father's absence loomed large enough to fill the house and swallow her whole. *Oh, Dad,* she thought miserably. *This can't be true.*

Ella felt Lucinda studying her. She forced herself to meet Lucinda's steady gaze. "So, it was just you and your father," Lucinda finally said. "No close relatives. No special family friends."

Ella felt a beat of gratefulness that Lucinda was, in fact, sensitive to her situation. "I guess that's what Dad wanted you to be," she confided. "He always felt it wasn't enough for me, just having him." She was hit with a fresh wave of grief.

Lucinda was nodding. "Well, dear, what do you intend to do?" she asked softly.

"Do?" Ella wasn't sure she understood her stepmother's question.

"Well, who will you live with? Who'll take care of you?" Lucinda's voice fairly oozed with sympathy. Ella was suddenly struck with the falsity of it. And with her stepmother's real meaning. "After all," Lucinda added, "we barely know each other, do we?"

Ella went cold with understanding. "But . . . but this is my home," she whispered incredulously.

Lucinda smiled. "Well, actually, dear, it's *my* home now. Your father did promise to provide for me. Oh, but of course, if you want to stay . . ."

Ella was speechless. She'd had her doubts about Lucinda, but she'd never imagined the woman to be quite as heartless as this. It was hardly a welcome invitation she'd extended. *An invitation!* Ella couldn't believe she was looking for an invitation to live in her own house! Her home—the only one she had ever known, the home that held memories of her mother, the home she and her father had shared after her mother was gone.

Ella looked over at Lucinda, leaning back in the armchair where her father used to sit. Lucinda's dark eyes were hard. The room was marked with her strong perfume and her icy presence. Ella could barely believe what was happening. She was a stranger in her own home. She felt numb. There had to be some mistake.

But as she looked at Lucinda's steely expression, she had to swallow against the terror rising in her throat. She was alone. Alone as she could ever be.

Prince Will basked in the glow from his computer. *Welcome, Will,* flashed the message on his screen. He smiled. Not "Your Royal Highness," not "Sir Will," not even Chris's teasing "Royal Willness." On-line, surfing the Internet, he was the same as anyone else. Plain old Will. He could travel anywhere, say anything.

Will knew his friends couldn't understand why

he'd turned down a chance to go into town to that new restaurant on Spruce Street. "There's this really cute waitress," Chris had said. "Maybe she has a friend."

Will had laughed. "Then, knowing you, maybe you'll get her friend's phone number, too."

"Fine. More for me," Chris had said. "Although I always do better when Your Willness is around. Good attention getter, you know? And all you have to do is sit there and be regal."

"Yeah, well, maybe next time." Will just wasn't up for the public eye tonight—the bodyguard he had to park by the door, the covert glances, a few outright stares. Sometimes Will didn't mind it. Occasionally he was even amused. Royal fever— here, in a country that professed to be immune to the whole idea of kings and queens! But tonight the lure of privacy was stronger than the pull of a night out.

Well, not exactly privacy. Actually, Will intended to do some serious socializing tonight. Maybe he'd log onto that comedy conference, hear some good jokes. Or visit that on-line museum. Or maybe he'd find someone who wanted to play a game of chess. Then again, he could just roam around, see what new stuff he'd wander into. No one had to know who he really was. No bodyguard, no palace protocol. No girls who only liked him for his royal crest.

Will glanced away from his computer and out his dorm-room window. A few twinkling stars studded an inky purple sky over the silhouette of rolling hills. Was it really such a fairy tale to think he might meet a girl like that? Someone who'd like him for who he was inside. He let himself imagine he was holding her under those stars. Her hair would be as light blond as the moon, or as purple-black as the sky—it didn't matter. But she'd be beautiful, and her eyes would shine with intelligence and love. He'd draw her even closer to him, his lips finding her soft lips.

Will sighed. He wasn't going to find a warm pair of lips behind his computer screen. But at least he could leave his Royal Willness behind for a while. . . .

Four

Home, sweet home. Ella wished she were headed somewhere else. Anywhere else. As she walked down the flagstone path to her house, the dark purple sky seemed somehow sinister, the stars piercingly sharp.

Ella had gone over to Steph's after school and stayed as long as she could. She didn't want to come home. *This place isn't mine anymore,* she thought as she approached the front door. Already there was new furniture replacing too many of the comfortable, gently worn pieces she'd grown up with—new chairs in the living room, a new dining-room set—all gleaming metal and glass, spare and cold like her stepmother and stepsisters.

She eased her key into the front-door lock and let herself in as quietly as she could. Maybe she could sneak up to her room without having to talk to any of them. Through the doorway to the living room, she could see Staci and Drew positioned in front of the glow of the television set. She quickly walked past the doorway and started up the wooden staircase on tiptoe.

But Lucinda's thin, raspy voice caught her. "Ella?" she called from the kitchen.

Ella froze. "Yes?"

"Ella, come here," her stepmother ordered. "I want to show you something."

Ella sucked in her breath and headed back down to the kitchen. What was it? Another piece of furniture? Some other new purchase? She pushed open the swinging door to the kitchen.

Lucinda sat at the table, smoking a cigarette. "Ella." The smoke curled up in snaky tendrils as she pronounced her name. Lucinda gestured at the sink with a sharp, pink nail. "You left the house this morning without doing the breakfast dishes. Where have you been, anyway?"

"With a friend," Ella said softly. "And I'm sorry, but I thought—well, I did the dishes after dinner last night, and the night before that, and I figured . . ." Her voice trailed off, thinking about her lazy stepsisters tubing out in the other room. Had either of them lifted a manicured finger since they'd come to live in this house? No, all they'd done was to make Ella feel that it was somehow her fault they'd had to move to a strange house, her fault they were sharing a room, her fault that she was underfoot, and that it was her job to make up for it. And Lucinda didn't help matters.

"You figured . . ." she mimicked. "Well, you figured wrong." She flicked an ash off her black dress. "I don't know what your father expected of you, but in *my* house, we all have to do our part."

Ella felt her muscles tense up. Why was her part so much more than anyone else's? Lucinda couldn't have been more obvious if she'd come right out and told Ella what a burden she was. *In my house . . . I don't know what your father expected of you. . . .* The ugly words hung in the smoky air. The house was filling up so fast with Lucinda's things that pretty soon there wouldn't be any sign of her father at all. Her father . . .

Ella felt sick with despair. Why did he have to go? Why did he have to leave her? And why had Lucinda married him if she was so quick to bury any trace of him. Ella knew the answer. Lucinda had as much as told her. She wanted to be taken care of, to be pampered—to get what she'd never had as a girl. And Dad—well, he'd always had a soft spot for others. A soft spot and a nice house and a secure, tidy savings he'd put away for the future.

Oh, Dad! Ella knew all he'd wanted was to give her a family—and to find a bit of companionship for himself. That was why he'd let himself be reeled in by Lucinda hook, line, and sinker.

"And by the way," Lucinda continued, "I'm having a few friends over tomorrow night. So your busy social life will have to be put on hold, got it? I'd like you home right after school to help out."

Ella felt her despair turn to shock. And anger. A party? Two weeks after her father had died? Two weeks after Lucinda had pledged to love him forever, and then lost him so suddenly? "Don't you think it's a little too soon after the funeral to be throwing parties?" Ella dared to say. Someone had to protect her father's memory.

Lucinda's pale face contorted in fury. "You little ingrate," she said, her words like a slap. "You're not the only person in this house in mourning. You're not the only one who hurts. My friends are coming to cheer me up. Do you understand?"

Ella felt dizzy. She breathed in Lucinda's perfume and smoke, saying nothing.

"And as for your friends," Lucinda went on, her voice low and threatening as thunderclouds. "Well, perhaps all your boyfriends are taken in by your looks and your perfect smile, but I'm not.

You can't get by on a pretty face and a good figure forever. Oh, I know girls like you think you can. You should be thankful to have a roof over your head, and instead you're acting as if I'm running a hotel for you. If you want to stay here, you will pitch in. Get it?"

Ella reached out, grabbing the back of one of the kitchen chairs to steady herself. In the living room, her stepsisters were doing nothing. Nothing at all. Ella took a deep breath, preparing to defend herself. If she wasn't welcome here, she'd leave.

But where would she go? she thought, and quickly snapped her mouth shut. What would she do? She had no job, no family, no other place to live. She looked around the kitchen. At least this room was still the same. The terra-cotta floor tiles her father had put down himself, the heavy wood table that Ella knew was still marked on the underside with her first set of crayons, the old-fashioned pegboard on the wall, hung with measuring spoons and cake molds and cookie cutters.

Ella had a faraway memory of making Christmas cookies with her mother, so many, many years ago. Rolling the buttery dough out on that very table, using the cookie cutters to make the shapes, and decorating them with shiny colored sugar. She thought of her mother's long, delicate hands arranging the cookies on a baking sheet. Ella swallowed back her tears.

This was her house. Hers. She wouldn't let Lucinda drive her out.

Lucinda was waiting for an answer. "I get it, Lucinda. I'll be home to help out tomorrow night," Ella said quietly. "And I don't have a boyfriend."

Lucinda's smile was sticky sweet. "I knew you'd understand, Ella dear." She took a long drag of her cigarette. "As long as you follow a few new rules, I'm sure we can all get along just fine."

"Ella! Hey, where've you been hiding?" Steph asked, catching up with her on the green lawn in front of school. "You have some secret romance going that I don't know about?"

Ella hiked her knapsack up on one shoulder. "In my dreams," she answered her friend.

It was crisp and sunny out, with a tang of fall. The very tips of some of the tree leaves had just begun to turn fiery colors. The sky was a cloudless deep blue directly overhead, fading to pale blue as it dipped toward the horizon. It was a beautiful day.

But Ella's mood was flat grey. "Lucinda's been

piling on the chores every single day this week," she told Steph.

"Oh, man. That stinks," Steph commiserated. "What does that woman have against you, anyway?"

Ella shrugged miserably. "She thinks I've had it so much easier than she ever did. I don't know what to do. I've tried to get along with her. I really have. And Staci and Drew—they're not a whole lot better."

"Sounds like pure jealousy," Steph said loyally. "They can doll themselves up as much as they want, and they still won't look half as good as you. And more important, they couldn't be a quarter as nice."

Ella smiled weakly. "Thanks, Steph."

They headed toward the entrance to school. Around them, kids talked and laughed, calling out to their friends, telling jokes. A few people sat on the front steps reading or looking over homework. Ella had barely found the time to do her own homework, after cleaning the house from top to bottom the previous night. She'd had to stay up much too late to finish her math, and today every bone, every muscle in her body felt tired. She swallowed hard.

"I don't know, Steph. I just don't know what to do."

Steph stopped walking. "Look, isn't there any-where else you could go? Any way out?"

Ella let out a long breath. "I've thought about it. Believe me, I can't *stop* thinking about it. But first I'd need to find a job, and then how could I support myself and stay in school at the same time? Plus, until I turn eighteen, I'm not even le-gally old enough to go off on my own."

Steph nodded slowly. "Well, listen, if it's any consolation, I told Jane Marston we'd go over to the flea market in Greenway this weekend. At least we'll get you outta that prison for the day."

"Yeah, well, we're supposed to drain and clean out the pool this weekend. Which probably means *I'll* do it, and *they'll* sit around stuffing their faces, telling me what to do. No, scratch that, Drew'll stuff her face. Staci and Lucinda will drink spring-water. And they'll all boss me around." Ella felt so far removed from the other kids jostling to get through the front doors to school, and so far away from even Steph. A day out with her friends . . . it should have been so simple. But in the space of a few weeks, it had become hopelessly out of reach.

"You'll find a way," Steph said tentatively. "But if you can't, will you mind if I went with Jane anyway?"

Ella bit her lip. She fought to hold back the

tears threatening to spill. "No." Her voice came out tight and stingy. "I mean, of course not."

Steph frowned. "Look, maybe you can get your chores done early, and we can go in the afternoon. You can't just give up, Ella." She took Ella's arm and gave her a little shake.

Ella felt the firm pressure of Steph's hand. And she had a flash of the busy, noisy Greenway flea market, row upon row of stands covering the town green, people selling everything from socks to cookware to antique furniture. Ella's father had taught her how to spot the best finds, wandering around patiently and sifting through piles of junk for the real gems. Last time she'd been there she'd found a sterling silver charm to add to her special charm bracelet—a tiny airplane with a propeller that actually spun around. The jangly silver bracelet had been a present from her mom on her sixth birthday, and she'd added a charm each year . . . until she'd died. Now Ella touched the airplane charm. If only that tiny plane could magically grow and take her away, far away. But Steph was right. She didn't want to give up.

"I'll see what I can do," Ella said. "Maybe if I rush home today and get the pool stuff started . . ."

"Great!" Steph said. "Wow, and here I was thinking you had some new, secret boyfriend.

Speaking of which, did you hear about Marly Parker and Kevin Carroll?"

As they walked toward their lockers, Ella listened to Steph go on about Marly and Kevin. How their parents hated each other, how they'd been sneaking around behind their backs. "Romeo and Juliet," Steph said. "Isn't it romantic? He had flowers delivered to her in homeroom yesterday."

"Cool. Were they roses?"

"A dozen of them. Red ones."

Ella tried to imagine herself getting a bouquet of red roses in Mrs. Hunter's homeroom, but the picture wouldn't come. Wasn't it only a few weeks ago that she'd been standing at her father's wedding, daydreaming about walking down the aisle herself? Feeling heady with romantic possibilities? Today she felt too tired for romance. Too tired for dreaming.

But Steph was right. She couldn't let Lucinda take away her dreams. She wouldn't.

Five

Straining her eyes in the waning daylight, Ella fished the last soggy leaf out of the pool with a long-handled net. A sliver of moon was already visible over the house, and one lone star dotted the sky like a beauty mark. Ella emptied the pile of leaves into a plastic garbage bag, laid the net down, and stretched out on one of the lounge chairs by the edge of the pool. She was taking a well-deserved break.

The one star twinkled overhead. Ella held it in her gaze and found herself thinking that old rhyme. *Star light, star bright, first star I see tonight . . .*

It had been a long time since she'd recited that poem, a long time since she'd wished upon a star. But if ever she needed a little magic, it was now. *Please let me go to the flea market with my friends tomorrow,* Ella whispered. No, wait. That was a waste of such a bright, silvery star. Maybe she should wish for something meatier. *Please let Lucinda and her daughters be nicer.* Fat chance. Ella stared at the star. Okay, maybe something more general. Like how about, *I wish that everything will turn out happily ever after.* Yes. Let the star magic take care of how. Ella gave a little laugh. Silly girl, she told herself. Playing a silly kid's game.

"Well, you certainly sound as if you're enjoying yourself." Lucinda's booming voice seemed to come out of thin air. Suddenly she was looming over Ella's chair.

Ella felt a trill of fear. She sat bolt upright. "Oh . . . I, uh, didn't see you coming."

"Well, here I am." The flare of Lucinda's lighter burned against the darkening sky. "I thought you were cleaning out the pool."

"I was. I am. I—I was just taking a break."

"I see." Lucinda drew a long drag of her cigarette, and the tip glowed like the evil twin of Ella's star. "I'm having a friend in from out of town this weekend," she said. "I expect you wouldn't mind giving up your room for a few days, would you?"

Ella felt her body go tight. Her room. The fluffy rug on the polished wood floors, the quilt her mother had made, the mobile of the elegant white seagull soaring through the air over the foot of her bed. Ella loved to watch the seagull's wings flap gently when a breeze blew in through an open window. Her room was the only place in the houses where she still felt at home.

"I seem to remember you saying that the attic was nice." Lucinda turned Ella's own words against her. "Good enough for one of my daughters, if I remember your suggestion correctly. And I believe there's an extra mattress up there, too."

Ella turned her eyes toward the house. And what about her stepsisters? The faint pulse of music floated out of Staci's and Drew's room. Lucinda must have followed Ella's gaze. "They've only barely unpacked. You can't expect them to move out as soon as they've gotten settled. Besides, there are two of them and only one of you. It's a reasonable solution."

Reasonable. Not that Ella seemed to have any other choice. She bit back her bitterness. *It's just for a couple of days,* she reminded herself. And if she managed to get away for part of the weekend, it wouldn't matter much, anyway. Yes, Ella had to get away. . . .

Ella summoned up a smile as bright and false as Lucinda's usually was. "I guess I don't mind. Just as you won't mind if I have a little time with my friends tomorrow."

Lucinda sucked on her cigarette.

"I'll make sure the house is spic-and-span for your guest," Ella added, for insurance.

She felt a flicker of surprise as Lucinda nodded slowly. "Well, okay, Ella. Oh, don't look so surprised. As long as you get all your chores done, I don't see why not . . ."

Ella waited until Lucinda turned and walked back across the lawn before allowing herself a small smile. Small but genuine. Maybe there was something to this star wishing after all.

Prince Will parked his books on his desk for the night and headed up to Hangout Central. H.C. was actually the TV lounge on the top floor of the boys' dorm, but half the time the old television wasn't even working. Though that never stopped anyone from post-study bull sessions and general goofing around up there. Besides, Will had a big-screen TV/VCR in his room. H.C. was strictly for company. He'd been spending too much time at his computer lately, too much time with faraway people and words on a screen. Sometimes even he needed to be around real, live people.

Will climbed the carpeted stairs, his footfalls silent, and pushed open the door at the head of the staircase.

"Yo, Will!" Kenny greeted him, looking up from a game of knee soccer as Will entered the large, shabby room.

Chris took full advantage of Kenny's pause in concentration to shuffle forward and jab the ball with his knee, sending it spinning along the brown indoor-outdoor carpet, past Kenny, and into an upended milk crate against the wall.

"Goal!" Chris shouted.

"Hey, no fair," Kenny said.

"Sure it is." Chris dug the ball out of the milk crate. "What's up, Will?"

Will shrugged. A couple of guys sat on the sofa, watching one of the first games of the pro basketball season. "Nothing much," Will said, dragging a chair over toward Chris and Kenny. He turned it around and sat down, his legs straddling the back of the chair. "So what's happening this weekend?"

"We were thinking that after practice tomorrow, we might head over and check out that flea market they have a few towns away," Chris said.

"Get me a new desk chair," Kenny said.

"What happened to your old one?" Will asked.

Kenny looked embarrassed. "Nothing, really," he mumbled.

Chris laughed. "He sat down in it. It totally collapsed on him. Yo, look alive!" Before Kenny knew what was happening, Chris shot another goal right by him.

"Man, I thought it was time-out," Kenny protested. "You keep cheating, and I'm going to stuff your head in that milk crate."

Will laughed. "Nice, friendly game up at H.C. tonight."

"So, you wanna come along tomorrow? Take a road trip?" Chris asked, retrieving the ball. "Maybe you can pick up some good bargains—a secondhand crown or a slightly used throne."

"You loser," Will said good-naturedly. "I know there's only one thing *you're* interested in picking up."

"Okay, guilty as charged. Maybe there'll be some cute girls wandering around there. Would that be so bad?" Chris asked.

"Just so long as you don't monopolize all the action," Kenny said.

Chris made a face. "Yo, Kenny, my man, don't blame me because you get tongue-tied around the lovely ladies. Besides, you know I can't be more than a sideshow when we've got His Princeliness around. It's that blue blood that really drives the girls mad with desire."

Will socked Chris in the arm. "Okay, okay, so maybe I'll never find a girl who loves me for my soul, like you guys do." He said it jokingly, but there was actually far too much truth in his statement.

"Aw, c'mon," Chris said. "You're making me blush!"

Will laughed. "Actually, though, a road trip sounds cool." Okay, so he probably wouldn't find his dream girl in the aisles of the flea market, but he wouldn't be sitting around moping about not finding her, either. "We can take my car."

"Great," Chris said, slapping Will on the back. "We were counting on it. Yo, what are you trying to pull?" he yelled at Kenny, just as Kenny was making a goal.

"I guess you're not as sharp with a ball as you are with the girls, buddy . . ."

Freedom is only a night away, Ella thought eagerly. She'd cleaned the pool until it was too dark to see. Then she'd vacuumed and dusted and scrubbed the house until it was spotless. She'd put fresh sheets on her bed for Lucinda's guests, and had put away everything on her desk.

Ella wiped the perspiration from her forehead with the back of her hand. She was exhausted, and it was beyond late. But Lucinda couldn't deny her some time out now.

She could see herself riding along in the sporty red car Steph's parents usually let her borrow. Steph at the wheel with her new driver's license, Ella up front, and Jane Marston in the back. The sunroof would be open, and they'd be cranking tunes on the CD player—something loud and fast, good driving music. Maybe they'd stop for a brunch at that tiny diner in Greenway with the great omelettes. Ella still had a little of the baby-sitting money she'd saved up this summer.

Heading toward the bathroom at the end of the hall, Ella peeled off her grimy clothes and stepped into a hot shower. The water felt wonderful. The steamy spray washed away the sound of Lucinda's angry voice and the thought of being locked up for even one more minute in this prisonlike house.

Ella drifted off in her daydreams as the water continued to pound on her back. She and Steph and Jane would shop and gossip and giggle. Just a normal day with the girls, which seemed like such a big deal, right now. A day off from her grief and loneliness, a day away from feeling like a servant in her own house, a day that was fun and easy.

Ella thought back to July. In the heat of the summer, she and Steph had driven out to the lake in Hammond State Park for the day. They'd swum halfway across the lake and back, sunbathed on the sand, and then swum some more. Later in the afternoon, they'd walked to the other end of the beach and run into Paul Sandler from school and some of his friends. They'd all wound up at Dairy Barn on their way home, laughing and flirting over slushies.

Ella hoped tomorrow would be as much fun. Who knew? Maybe she'd even meet someone in the stands at the flea market. Maybe they'd both be bargaining over the same old movie poster or funky souvenir.

Ella took her time soaping up, letting the steam seep into her tired body. Dad had died only a month ago, but it felt like so much longer since she'd been a regular high-school girl. As she rinsed off, she imagined her old self emerging like a butterfly from a soapy cocoon.

She dried off and slipped into a cozy flannel nightgown.

The knock on the door was like a blast of cold water. "Ella?" Lucinda didn't wait for an answer to barge right in. "Good, I'm glad I caught you before you went to sleep. The house looks very nice, dear."

Ella felt a guarded beat of surprised satisfaction.

"Now I'm sure you'll do just as good a job up in the attic tomorrow," Lucinda went on.

Ella felt her good feelings vanishing into tension. No. She wasn't going to let Lucinda ruin her plans. "Okay," she said quietly. "I'll work on it when I get home tomorrow."

Lucinda shook her head. "I don't think so. There's a lot to do up there. All those boxes and things just thrown around. It could take all day."

"But you said I could spend some time with my friends." Ella protested.

"I said if you finished your chores." Lucinda gave a nasty smile.

Ella couldn't stop a fat tear—and then another—from stinging her cheeks. "It's not fair," she said, crying. "It's just not fair."

Lucinda gave a shrug, her shoulders bony and sharp under her silky bathrobe. "*Life* is not fair sometimes, Ella. I didn't ask to be born into nothing. I didn't ask to be widowed again as soon as I'd remarried. I didn't ask to have another person to feed and shelter. My dear, you're lucky you have a roof over your oh-so-pretty little head. Do you know that?"

Ella pushed past Lucinda and raced up to the

attic, her bare feet pounding the stairs. She flung herself on the thin mattress in the middle of the floor and just sobbed. Tears soaked the sheet quickly. She felt as if she might never stop crying. It was no use. Unless she wanted to be out on the street, she was a prisoner in her own house.

Six

Ella awoke to sunshine pouring in a slant through the high attic windows. It splashed puddles of warm light on the pine floor, and fell on the boxes and trunks and dust-covered odds and ends that cluttered the room. The faintly musty smell carried a powerful sense of all the old memories that were stored up there. Ella sat up and gave a catlike stretch. The hopelessness she had felt the night before was loosening its hold on her. It was so quiet, so peaceful in the attic, the exposed beams and rafters under the roof giving it a cozy cabinlike air. And it was far from the rest of the house.

Ella yawned lazily. There in one corner was her mother's old one-speed bicycle, with the worn leather seat and the wicker basket still suspended from the handlebars. And next to it, the top of Ella's sled peeked out from behind a stack of boxes—her childhood Flexible Flyer with the fire-engine-red metalwork that she used to drag over to the hill behind the elementary school whenever it snowed.

Ella stood up and peered out a window. It was a nice day for a road trip. Steph and Jane were lucky. But Ella's anger seemed to have lost its sharp nighttime edge. Maybe it was waking up to all those mementos from her past.

Ella wandered over to one side of the attic and peered into an open box. It was stuffed with letters and papers. The edge of a snapshot stuck out of an envelope filled with photos. Ella bent down and reached in, taking out the photos. From the top of the pile, her mother and father smiled out at her, young and full of life, the ocean waves breaking behind them on the shore of a long white-sand beach.

Oh, Mom, Dad. I miss you both so much.

Ella was touched by a bittersweet kind of warmth. The spirit of her parents and her past filled this room. Lucinda had no idea that she'd sent Ella to a place of happy memories. Ella sat down cross-legged and riffled through more of the pictures. Mom and Dad posing in front of their first car, a tiny yellow Volkswagen. Ella laughed, remembering her parents saying how that car had been nothing but trouble from the day they'd bought it. "The right color for a lemon, too," her father had once said. More beach photos. Ella's mother, with the sun setting into the water behind her.

Treasure. That's what was up here. Ella's own family treasure. Letters she'd written home from camp the summer she was twelve, her old close-and-play phonograph and a box of children's records. *Tubby the Tuba* had been her favorite. She found herself humming out loud. She could still remember how the tuba part went.

Her father's college track trophies, boxes of old clothes, ice skates that were too small. . . .

Lucinda could never take all these memories away. Ella felt a rush of optimism. Yes, she had her past. And she had her future too. She couldn't lose sight of that. Ella was going to match the new day with a new attitude. Okay, so she was missing out on the flea market. A great day with Steph and Jane. A fun time. But it was just one day. One day, she reminded herself. If she'd let herself feel defeated, Lucinda would have won.

Ella knew she wasn't going to be under Lucinda's spell for the rest of her life. No, of course not. She had one more year of high school, and then she would graduate. She'd be eighteen years old. Legal and free. Ella could still look forward to so many things: college, a career, love. She'd apply for a scholarship, take out a loan, work her way to a college degree. People did it.

She imagined herself walking across the quad of a college campus, ivy-covered stone buildings, brick walkways, perhaps a church bell tolling off in the distance. She'd be heading toward her favorite class—history or geology or maybe sociology—something where the world was open before her. And of course she'd be walking arm-in-arm with that special guy, the one whose face she couldn't quite see yet. . . .

No, she wouldn't be under Lucinda's power forever.

"Cool sweater," Chris said to the pretty dark-skinned girl who was pulling a pink beaded cardigan out of a bin of vintage clothes. The girl, trolling for bargains with a tall, equally attractive friend, looked up and glanced at Chris neutrally. He gave her a friendly, mild smile that melted the distance between them.

She smiled back. "You think?" She held the sweater up to herself. The deep rose color set off her dark chocolate eyes and hair. She posed a split second for Chris before turning to her friend for her opinion.

"Looks great, Jane," her friend said.

Chris nodded his agreement. "Good color on you."

"Look over there. It's gross how easy it is for Chris to meet a girl," Will commented to Kenny. They stood a short distance from Chris, by a long table loaded with secondhand books.

"How'd you know what I was thinking?" Kenny asked.

Will shrugged. "'Cause I have the same problem as you." He tried to imagine himself going up to a girl he didn't know and starting a conversation that way. He was too self-conscious about being His Royal Willness to act so casual. Most of the time, girls tended to get nervous around him, or they really tried to show off. It was his title. "It's hard for me to tell what most girls are thinking or what they're really like half the time," he commented to Kenny.

Chris continued to flirt comfortably with the pink-sweater girl. Her friend wandered over to the far end of the book table to peruse the dusty titles.

"Half the time?" Kenny echoed. "Man, that sounds like a pretty good record to me. Way good. I'm 0-for-0."

"That's because you don't even try," Will said. "You gotta lose some of your shyness."

Kenny frowned slightly. "I'm not a stud muffin like Chris. Or a prince like you. I mean, girls might get self-conscious and stuff around you, but at least they recognize you. Me, it's like I'm not even here. You'd think I took up too much space for anyone to miss me, wouldn't you?"

Will laughed. "I think it's mostly in your head, man. That girl over there—the sweater girl's friend—she's looking right at you." The girl had glanced up from the rows of books, and her gaze went briefly to Kenny. "Say something to her," Will encouraged softly.

"Um, ah—like what?" Kenny's voice cracked nervously.

"Like—well . . . Any good books down at that end?" Will called out.

The girl looked over at Will, and then at Kenny again. "Hi. So . . . uh, what kind of books do you guys like?" she called back comfortably.

"See? Only half the time," Kenny said, with an edge of jealousy.

"Yo, thickhead, she's talking to you, too," Will said under his breath. He gave Kenny a poke in his side. Kenny shuffled his feet and cleared his throat, but he didn't say anything.

Suddenly Will felt another pair of eyes on him. The girl Chris had been talking to was staring at him intensely. She raced over to her friend, still clutching the pink sweater, and whispered something to her. Will didn't have to wonder what she'd said. He saw his celebrity mirrored in the girls' expressions. The girl who'd asked what he liked to read bit her lip, and her cheeks got red. *Darn,* Will thought. He shouldn't have said anything at all.

He tried to act as if nothing had happened, covering up the girls' flustered giggling by saying something—anything. "Well, I like to read pretty much everything, if it's good," he said, trying hard to keep up the casual banter. "Fiction, biographies, mysteries . . ." But as Will continued to ramble on about his favorite books and what he'd read, he suddenly noticed a man pointing a camera in his direction, and several more people who began to hover about. His bodyguard moved him away as a small crowd was beginning to form.

"Oh, my heavens!" Will heard a woman's voice say. "Isn't that . . . Oh! It is! Larry, do you know who that boy over there is?"

"Um, Kenny, you want to take off? How about some lunch?" Will asked. "Yo, Chris!" He motioned that they were heading out.

Chris shrugged. "Okay. Sure."

Before the crowd had a chance to get any bigger, Will led his friends away, in search of a more private spot. "Good-bye," he called to the girl looking through the books.

"Maybe we'll catch you later," Chris added to her friend.

Will gave a half-laugh to himself. *Catch you later.* Nothing *that* casual ever rolled off his tongue to a girl. A prince didn't catch a girl later. A prince dated. Formally, and with fanfare, whether he wanted it or not. And lights, camera, action, crowds—it was part of his royal obligation. But how could he get through all that to find out what a girl was really like? How could he borrow some of that breezy, easy attitude that came so naturally to Chris?

He felt a pinch of loneliness. Funny how it was all the attention that made him feel most alone. At times like these, he almost wished he could be a nobody for a while.

Ella balanced her lunch tray as she scanned the school cafeteria for Steph. Over by the windows, some of the guys from the football team were practicing passes with hot-dog buns, a definite opening to a full-scale food fight. The burnouts were in their usual dark corner of the room, and center stage, George Berk, notorious class clown, was entertaining a growing audience with his exaggerated pantomimes of different teachers. Ella watched for a moment as he hiked his pants up over an imaginary bulging belly and shuffled over to an invisible chalkboard where he began writing with large, florid gestures. Ella laughed to herself. Mr. McCann! She'd had him last year for Algebra II, and George had gotten him just right.

Ella looked to see if Steph was part of the crowd watching him. She searched for Steph's familiar brown curls and tall, willowy frame, but she didn't spot her. Steph wasn't sitting with Susan Peters and her friends from the girls' basketball team, either. Oh, there she was, near the door, her head bent toward Jane Marston's. As Ella carried her lunch over to them, she could hear them laughing even before she reached them.

"Hey, guys," Ella said, sliding her tray onto the table.

Steph and Jane looked up.

"Oh, wow, Ella, you missed it!" Jane said immediately. "You'll never guess who we saw at the flea market this weekend."

Steph jumped right in. "The prince!" she said, with a touch of breathlessness. "Prince William of

Montroig. Oh, Ella, he's incredibly handsome. And guess what? I was looking through the same stall of old books as he was, and he and his friend actually said hi to me. I mean, he talked to me. To me! He asked me what I liked to read, and told me his all-time favorite book was *One Hundred Years of Solitude*. And he read it in the original Spanish! He speaks, like, four languages fluently."

"And he has a really cute smile," Jane said with a giggle. "Kind of lopsided and friendly, like he was, well—a regular guy, or something."

"Except he's a prince!" Steph giggled, too.

Ella sat down next to Steph. She couldn't help a tickle of envy. So much for her own daydreams about rubbing elbows with a special guy at the Greenway market. It was Steph and Jane who'd gotten to flirt with a real, live prince. And one who loved one of her own favorite books, too. Ella pushed her franks and beans around on her plate with her plastic fork.

"One of his friends was pretty cute, too," Jane commented. "Curly blond hair, tall, handsome face . . ."

"Yeah, and he totally liked you," Steph said to Jane. "I mean, you could have picked a real rag out of that clothing bin, and he would have thought it looked nice on you."

Jane looked embarrassed and shook her head.

"Nah. It's just that dark pink really is my color."

"Oh, right. And that's why he was following you around and flirting wtih you and stuff. Just because pink is your color."

Jane laughed. "Oh, wow, and speaking of following people around, how about that big guy in the suit—the prince's bodyguard? Can you imagine having someone trailing after you like that, all the time? Like a permanent chaperon, or something?"

Ella listened to Steph and Jane replaying the highlights of their day together. She took a tiny bite of hot dog, but it tasted like cardboard. She wasn't really hungry, anyway. There was no escaping how left out she felt.

She and Steph had been best friends since elementary school. Steph had even known Ella's mother. They'd spent Thanksgivings together, both families, and Steph and Ella had insisted on going to the same summer camp and sharing a bunk.

But today it was Steph and Jane. Jane and Steph. Thick as thieves after a day that Ella had missed out on. Ella knew it wasn't Steph's fault she hadn't been able to go along. But that didn't make it hurt any less.

The future, Ella reminded herself. There's still the future. But while she was waiting for the future, she hoped the present wasn't passing her by.

Seven

Ella raced up to her room, determined to slam the door behind her and shut out the rest of a house that was no longer hers. Instead, she found Drew panting and puffing, struggling to get a large, overstuffed suitcase in through Ella's bedroom door. Staci watched from the hallway, one hand on a bony hip.

"What's going on?" Ella asked. She was sure that with Staci and Drew involved, she wasn't going to like the answer.

Drew looked up and wiped a thin line of sweat from above her lips. "Oh, good. It's about time. You can help me with this, Ella. And you'll have to clear your stuff out so I have room to put mine in."

"Excuse me?" Ella felt her uneasiness swelling.

"Yeah, Mother's guest left this morning," Staci said, as if that explained everything.

"And what does that have to do with all this junk?" Ella prompted nervously. "This is still my room."

Drew looked to Staci, and Staci nodded. "Actually, the attic's your room now," Drew said matter-of-factly.

"But that was just for the weekend—just while your mother's guest was here," Ella protested.

"That's what you thought," Staci said, sharing a conspiratorial smile with Drew. "I mean, you can't honestly expect me to share a room with *her*—" she gave a dismissive wave at her sister "—just because my mom got married to some dead guy."

Ella felt a stab of intense pain. How could Staci talk about her father like that?

"Why do you hate me so much?" Ella asked softly.

Drew stopped tugging on her suitcase. She raised an eyebrow. "We don't," she said, a shrug of her shoulders making it clear that she simply couldn't care less. "But why should you have your own room and not me? Besides, you like it up in the attic. We all heard you say so, right, Stace?"

"You know, you've still got tons more stuff left in my room," Staci said by way of answering her sister.

Ella was overcome by powerlessness. "And your mother said you could just toss me out? Oh . . . never mind." Even if Lucinda hadn't given them permission, she certainly wouldn't stop Staci and Drew from doing it now.

"Hurry up, Drew," Staci ordered. "I want to do some rearranging in my room, and I need you out. Hey, maybe you'll even drop a couple of pounds lugging that stuff around. You could use the workout."

Drew shot her sister a dirty look. "Just because I don't think half a carrot's a huge meal . . . Anyway, I can't really do anything until Ella moves her junk out."

Staci frowned. "Okay, so, Ella, move your oh-so-pretty behind. I'm sure you do it for the boys all the time."

A clack of hard heels on the staircase announced Lucinda's arrival. Ella turned to see her coolly taking in the scene. She held her breath, hoping Lucinda would ask Drew what she thought she was doing. Even if she secretly knew she was as good as banished to the attic already.

Lucinda gave the merest hint of an icy smile. "And while you're at it, Ella, you might as well box up your father's clothes and bring them up there with you. I could use more room in my closet." She clicked away toward her bedroom without waiting for an answer.

Ella saw Drew and Staci exchange a satisfied look—a moment of meanness at someone else's expense rather than at their own.

Ella fought back her tears. She'd had too many bouts of crying recently. Way too many, and she didn't want her stepsisters to see how much they'd gotten to her. Ella stepped around Drew's suitcase and tried not to think too hard about anything. She began pulling clothes out of her chest of drawers and stuffing them into the duffel bag she used to take to summer camp when she was younger.

The worst part was that Ella wasn't sure it even mattered anymore if Drew took over the cozy room that had been Ella's all her life. What good was a room in a house with no love? All Ella really wanted was to find a way out.

Ella sat in English class, chewing on the end of her pencil. She couldn't concentrate on the poem they were reading—something about star-filled watermelons. Her own lucky star had failed her. Her hands were raw and chapped from all the cleaning and housework her stepmother had been piling on. Ella was head dishwasher, cleaner, plant waterer, and errand girl. She did the laundry. She ironed her stepsisters' clothes. Yesterday she'd even sewn a button on Drew's skirt.

"Just a tiny favor," Drew had said, with a saccharine smile. Ella had hesitated. "Because someone is fortunate to have shelter and food in her stomach, right, mother?"

And then Drew had complained that Ella had sewn it too tight. "Can't you do anything right?" As if it were Ella's fault that Drew had a way of putting too much food in her stomach. Ella had ended up ripping off the button and sewing it on all over again.

When company came, Ella wasn't even introduced anymore. Just ordered around like a servant. As for pocket money, new shoes, a book . . . that was out of the question. She'd spent the last of her summer baby-sitting savings on a new diary she'd barely written in. She'd hoped it might help to have someplace to write out her feelings—her sorrow, her anger, her fear. But she was always too tired to get to it.

And what would she write on those clean white pages, anyway? That the future was a dense woods and she couldn't see through the forest of obstacles. That she couldn't imagine how she'd possibly pay for college. That there was no money even for application fees. And no time to work on those applications, let alone get her homework done. She was so tired. So very sad. Ella slumped down behind her desk and felt her eyes closing. If only her father hadn't left her all alone. . . . If only her luck hadn't run out. . . .

This time last year, she was going to school football games with Steph, screaming her lungs out for their team—and giggling about whether the home or the visiting team had the hottest players. Not that you could really tell with all that equipment they were hidden under.

Ella remembered how after one game, Steph had talked her into waiting by the door to the visitors' locker room so they could try to meet one of the players. From the field, he'd looked good enough for Steph to develop a massive crush on him. But postgame and closeup, his extra-loud voice and obnoxious attitude had sent Steph sneaking away, looking as if she'd just tasted something rotten.

"Teach you to root for someone on the other team!" Ella had teased her.

Steph. Ella let out a long, silent breath. Steph had been so buddy-buddy with Jane Marston since their trip to the Greenway flea market. Of course it didn't help that every time Steph wanted to do something, Ella was busy scrubbing or serving, or she was just too unhappy to muster up a bright face and take part in the normal things a teenage girl liked to do. It was hard enough just to try to pull herself through a day.

Ella felt a sudden jolt of anger that her father had left her to this. Left her without anyone to turn to. Left her in the clutches of Lucinda and her nasty daughters. How had Dad been so easily blinded by that woman's sleek looks and cool charade of sophistication? Why didn't he see what was underneath? Ella could feel her body trembling. Why had her father deserted her this way?

Dad. Oh, Dad. Her anger mixed with an ache of loneliness. And she was overcome by it. She missed her dad. Oh, how she missed him. Never again would they walk in the woods behind their house as the trees turned bright with fall, or tender green with spring. They wouldn't experiment with a new recipe for dinner ever again—getting the hard part right, but burning the rice. He wouldn't ask her how her day had been, or help her with her homework. She wouldn't help him pick out the right tie for some important meeting or other. They wouldn't—

"Ella! Ella Browning!" Mrs. Pearl's voice cut into her reverie. Ella's eyes flew open. "Ella, would you like to tell the class how a poem about something as ordinary as a watermelon can become an ode?"

Ella looked down at the copy of the poem on her desk. She hadn't heard a word of what Mrs. Pearl had been saying. And what was the definition of an ode? She thought she remembered Mrs. Pearl saying something about it at the beginning of class, but she couldn't recall what. "I, um—" She felt all eyes on her as she tried to skim the poem on the spot. Someone in the back of the room snickered.

"We're waiting," Mrs. Pearl said. "If I'd wanted a poem to put you to sleep, I would have chosen a lullaby. . . ." There were a few giggles around the classroom. Ella could feel her cheeks burning. "Maybe someone else can answer the question," the teacher finally said. "Ella, do I need to remind you that you're on the verge of failing? I'd advise you to pay attention if you want to graduate."

And then the teacher was calling someone else's name, but her words reverberated in Ella's mind. *Pay attention if you want to graduate. . . .* Ella blinked back a stray tear. Last year she'd been an honor-roll student. Last year, her teachers had had nothing but praise for her work. This year, the teachers who knew about her father were just letting her slide. And the ones who didn't, like Mrs. Pearl, were just about ready to give up on her.

Forget college. Forget the scholarship. Forget getting out of the house. Ella might not even get through her last year of high school. The future was so dark, it was disappearing completely.

Eight

Ella sat at the kitchen table, sneaking a look at the poem they'd read in English class that day— the one about the watermelon. Initially she'd been scared into it by Mrs. Pearl's warning about her failing. But Ella soon found the printed words working on her senses, until she actually felt the heat of summer, despite the new chill in the air outside. She had a sudden thirst for the sweet coldness of the poet's watermelon, described in vivid images and rich language.

Ella kept an ear tuned for Lucinda's return, ready to chuck the book in the nearest cabinet and grab a sponge. Ella was supposed to be cleaning the oven while Lucinda was out getting her nails done. The oven! Lucinda probably couldn't even handle a batch of slice-and-bake cookies.

Ella went back to the beginning of the poem

and began to read it again. Blue skies and scorched shoes, hot stones and swelling fruit, stars and rubies and wild rivers—the page was filled with color and shimmer and movement. And all to describe something as deliciously simple as biting into a slice of watermelon.

Ella sighed. She'd almost forgotten what it was like to take pleasure in those extra-important small things in life. The thirst of the poem was her own thirst for how good life could be. Except that there was no elegantly simple solution for Ella.

She laughed sadly to herself. If only a bite of watermelon could solve her—

Tap, tap.

A noise at the kitchen door made her jump. Ella immediately tossed her book under the table and looked up guiltily. But instead of catching sight of Lucinda's pale, sharp features, she could see a round-faced woman, shabbily dressed, but with a sweet smile. She looked familiar, and it took Ella a moment to place her. Oh, that was it— she was the woman who came around every year before the holidays, collecting food and clothes for the needy. Ella's father had always donated generously.

Ella went over to the door. She hadn't even given a thought to the holidays. In fact, until now she hadn't even remembered they were almost here. A couple of weeks until Thanksgiving. Then Christmas and New Year's. What did they mean with no family to help her celebrate? This year the holidays would surely bring nothing but extra work and extra loneliness. Ella couldn't help feeling sorry for herself as she opened the door.

"Hello, child," the woman greeted her. "I'm here taking up my annual collection for those less fortunate. Food, clothing—anything you can spare would be much appreciated."

Ella's first thought was to tell the woman that she was now one of those less-fortunate souls. Her second thought was that she should be ashamed of herself. The woman at her door was dressed in a threadbare cardigan, an old, floppy hat, and worn-out slacks. She couldn't have had much more than those for whom she was collecting. Yet she wanted to help. Ella had a place to live, three meals a day. That much she hadn't lost. There were those who had it so much worse than she did.

"I know I've always been able to count on you and your father for support," the woman said, giving Ella another sweet smile.

Ella tried not to get pulled under by another tug of self-pity. "My father . . . he . . . passed away," she stammered.

The woman frowned. "Oh. Oh, my. I'm so sorry. So deeply sorry. He seemed like a good man, your father."

Ella nodded. "He was." She wanted to give this nice lady something in her father's memory. But what was hers to give anymore? The rooms were filled with Lucinda's furniture. The closets were filled with—wait a minute! What about Dad's closet? And all his clothes that Lucinda had made Ella bring up to the attic.

"You know, I'm sure—well—my father wouldn't want his clothing to be collecting dust when someone else could use it."

She felt a rush of sadness at the thought of giving Dad's things away. It was so—final. But she knew he would have wanted her to do it. And come to think of it, there were tons of leftovers in the refrigerator from Lucinda's latest social gathering. Fancy catered goodies from the best shop in town that were just going to waste because Lucinda and the girls preferred to eat out. Ella could donate those to the woman's collection, too.

"Why don't you to come in?" Ella asked, opening the door wider. She prayed Lucinda would stay away a while longer.

"Why, thank you." As the woman stepped inside, she put a gentle hand on Ella's arm. "Does the sad news mean you're living here all alone now?"

"If only that were true!" Ella couldn't stop the words from rushing out. She saw the woman's brow crease. "See, I'm living here with my step-mother and stepsisters. . . ." she explained, her voice trailing off. She shouldn't be burdening a total stranger with her problems.

The woman looked searchingly at Ella and held her gaze. Her eyes were blue and caring. Her face was ever so slightly lined. She was neither young nor old—perhaps about the age Ella's mother would have been if she'd been alive. "I do see," she said. "I do see, my dear."

When was the last time anyone had called her "dear" and it had sounded so sincere? Ella found her eyes welling up with tears.

"Oh, child, don't despair," the woman said. "Sometimes there is a happily ever after. You must believe that."

Ella was startled. *Happily ever after*. Those were the very words she'd used when she'd wished upon that star. How could this woman have known that? Oh, but it was just an expression. And her words were just words. Kind ones, yes, but Ella would need more than that to end up happily ever after.

"I hope you're right," she said quietly. "Now, let's see what we can put together to give you."

Lucinda came speeding up the gravel driveway just as the woman was pulling away in her rust-spotted van. Ella watched as they squeezed their vehicles past each other. She had the momentary sensation of having just helped pull off a heist, the loot safely in the back of the van that was taking off down the road and out of sight. At least Lucinda would see it that way—Ella was sure. Even though the loot consisted of few boxes of clothes that were just taking up space, and some leftover food.

Ella steeled herself as Lucinda got out of her flashy blood-red sports car, her high black boots emerging first, followed by the rest of her chic black-clad frame.

"What was that eyesore doing in my driveway, Ella?" Lucinda slammed her car door. "Someone you know paying a visit?"

Ella decided to tell her the truth. After all, how could Lucinda treat her any worse than she already did. "She comes around every year to collect for the needy," Ella said. "Right before the holidays."

"Well. How good of her," Lucinda commented acidly.

"My father always gave whatever he could."

"Oh, did he?" Lucinda headed toward the house. "But your father's not here to help anyone anymore, is he?" Her voice was bitter.

Ella trailed after her. "Actually, I was able to make one last donation from him."

Lucinda stopped walking. "Excuse me? Are you saying you gave away something that belonged to me?"

Ella shook her head. "Not to you. To my father. You said yourself that his clothes were taking up space and you wanted me to bring them up to the attic. I thought someone else might be able to use them. And some of the leftovers from your party—they would have gone bad. . . ."

Lucinda's face grew tight with anger. "Now listen here, young lady, and listen well. This is my house now. Mine. You do not do anything under my roof without my permission. You think we have so much that we can simply give things away? Your father promised to take care of me, and then he left me with more mouths to feed than I had before. You feel for the needy? Is that it?"

"I just thought—" Ella wished she'd kept quiet. Lucinda wouldn't have even noticed she'd given away her father's things. "In the spirit of the holiday season . . ."

"Well, perhaps you'd like to see what it's like to have nothing," Lucinda raged. "It's something I know only too well. You want to give things away? Let's start with your own clothes. How would you like to give them away?"

Ella felt a shiver of misery. Give away her clothes? Lucinda couldn't mean it. But one look at Lucinda's face told her how wrong she was.

"Oh, please, Lucinda," she pleaded. "My father's clothes—no one was using them. I thought you didn't want them. I'm sorry I didn't ask you first. It won't happen again. I promise."

Lucinda took her time answering. "It had better not," she said.

Did that mean she was off the hook? That her wardrobe was safe? Ella allowed herself a breath of relief.

Lucinda pushed open the front door and looked over her shoulder. "Now let's go take a look in your closet and see how you're going to help out all those poor, needy people."

Ella felt her heart sink.

"In the spirit of the holiday, dear," Lucinda added with a smooth, oily smile.

Nine

"And merry Christmas to you, too," Prince Will said with displeasure. He slapped the letter he was holding with the back of his free hand.

"What's wrong, Sir Will?" Chris, holding a thin pile of magazines and envelopes, joined him at his box in the Chason mail room.

Will shrugged. "Holiday parties," he grumbled.

Chris arched an eyebrow. "Parties? So what's the problem? Hey, Tricia," he said as a pretty redhead in running tights and sneakers passed by. "Catch you tonight?"

Tricia nodded and smiled, giving a little wave to Will, too. Will had dated her roommate, Sophie, a few times the year before. He waved back distractedly. He wished he didn't have to go home for Christmas at all.

"Yes!" Chris said as she walked away. "Date

with the best pair of legs ever to run cross-country track."

Will shook his head. "Man, maybe your relationships would last longer if you could get a focus on the whole person rather than just the legs, or the face or the . . . whatever." Chris's attitude was a little too close to having a girl fall for Will only because he was a prince.

But Chris just laughed. "Mmm. Trish has a nice whatever, too. Now what were you saying about holiday parties? You have a few invitations?"

Will nodded. "A few. Like from every organization in my country, for starters. And from every person who has some claim to some title—Mr., for instance," he joked morosely. "And it's my duty to attend every single event I can cram into my vacation. If you can call it that."

"You're a regular party animal. Tough life, bud," Chris said.

Will felt a tickle of annoyance. "Look, it would be nice to just sit around one day and read a book, or take a hike on the spur of the moment. Okay, I know the social events come with my position," he allowed. "That's not really the problem."

"So?" Chris asked. He and Will headed through the mail room, toward the doors to central campus.

"So, along with the list of events I'll be attending, my mother has sent a list of the girls I'll be escorting," Will explained.

"Hel-lo? First you're moaning about parties, and now you're moaning about girls at the parties? Maybe I should take a trip to the royal estate in your place. You could stay here . . . and have your head examined, pal!"

"You just don't understand," Will said.

"Apparently not."

Will glanced at the page in his hand. There it was. Printed up and already decided. But Will couldn't get excited about a single one of his dates. "Look," he said to Chris, as they stepped outside. He blinked in the bright, crisp fall sunlight. "Trish is pretty cute, huh?"

"You got that right. Pretty and cute."

"And despite your comment about her legs, I bet you think she's someone you might really like."

"I do really like her. She's gorgeous."

"You idiot. I mean her personality—when you get to know her."

"Oh, okay. Yeah, she's seems pretty cool. But don't go spreading around that I told you. I wouldn't want to ruin my pigheaded reputation."

Will laughed. "Don't worry. So let's say I told you that instead of going out with Trish tonight, you had to go out with—let's see . . . Oh, I know. Jessie Adair."

"Oh, man! You mean that one in English class? Huge head, body like a toothpick? Madly in love with the sound of her own voice? Corrects the teacher?"

"Yeah, her."

"No way, Will. I'd rather become a monk."

"Not a job that would suit you very well," Will said. "But you get what I'm saying. What if someone decided for you who you were going to date?"

The fallen leaves under their feet crackled as they crossed beneath the bare branches of a sprawling maple. "Come on, Will. The girls in that letter can't be close to as bad as Jessie Adair."

Will squinted to read the printed names in the bright daylight. "Edith Jasper Highsmith. The world's biggest snob. Probably thinks she's too good to be princess of my tiny country. Patricia Marchand. She's sweet, but she's totally afraid of her own shadow. Try taking her on a long hike in the woods. Elsa Von Dussel. Face like a horse, but her father's some important count. Lady Jane Valle. Pure as the driven snow, and about as cold. I could get more comfort and warmth from my pillow. Oh, okay—Sarah Rawlings. She's a nice girl. Pretty, too, but I didn't choose her."

"Yeah, I get it." Chris finally gave in.

"This is supposed to be like a test drive for the right bride," Will added. "My mother's list of suitable young ladies." He put his hands around his neck and made a choking sound.

"So what are you going to do about it?"

Will let out a breath of resignation, like air escaping from a deflating balloon. "I guess I'll be as nice as I can be to Edith and Elsa and the whole pack of them. And when I go to sleep, I'll dream about some really incredible girl I'll probably never find."

They followed a narrow walkway toward the dining hall. "His Willness disappoints me," Chris said. "I thought you were more romantic than that. You can't just give up."

"You have a better idea?" Will asked.

They walked in silence for a few moments. Then Chris let loose a triumphant, "Yes!" He pumped his arm in the air.

Will felt a breeze of optimism. "Tell me."

"Okay. We'll throw a huge party. Rent out The Overlook. Great scenery, food, dancing. Live band. The works. We'll invite everyone. Not just from Chason, but from town, too. All those cute girls you see around the mall and at the movie theater and when you go out for coffee or a slice of pizza.

Yeah, we'll invite every single girl in the county. And out of all those girls, there she'll be. You'll see her from across the room, and you'll just know she's the one. Your eyes will meet. The two of you will sort of drift together, fall into each other's arms as a slow song is playing . . ."

Will's laughter rose in the cool air. "Which one of us is the hopeless romantic again? Not that that sounds so bad. But listen, what if I don't meet her? Then what?"

Chris raised his shoulders. "Then we'll still throw the party of the year, and it'll be a blast. If you're going wind up married to Patricia Von-what's-her-face, you better get your fun in now."

It was all anyone could think about. Prince William's Christmas bash. The event of the year. Ella passed a group of girls standing in a knot by the water fountain.

"I just bought this totally amazing deep green ball gown," Ella heard one of them saying. Ella walked by them quickly, trying to suppress the wave of jealousy she felt.

"Oh, my God, I'm so excited. I can't wait for the weekend," she heard a girl who'd been in her math class the year before saying to a friend. "Do you think we'll get to dance with the prince?"

Ella set her mouth and squared her shoulders. She wasn't going to pay attention to all the party talk. She headed toward her locker. But she stopped in her tracks as she spotted Steph and Jane down the hall talking excitedly. She didn't have to hear them to know what the conversation was about. What they were going to wear to the party. How they were going to do their hair. Whether or not to splurge on that new miniskirt at the mall. How they were going to get the prince to notice them.

Steph looked up for a moment. Ella began to raise her hand to wave. But as Steph turned back to Jane, she dropped her arm to her side. She frowned and did an about-face, hurrying away down the hall. Had Steph seen her? Was she ignoring her? Ella didn't feel all that comfortable with Steph these days, anyway. Oh, they still sat with each other at lunch—with Jane, too. And Steph continued to invite Ella over after school, but it had gotten to be a mere formality. They both knew Ella wouldn't be able to make it, and that Jane would go instead.

Steph and Jane. Ella wondered if Steph would do Jane's long chestnut hair in a French braid for the big party, the way she had sometimes done for Ella. Or if she and Jane would stay up all night afterward, eating cheese popcorn and trading details on every minute of the evening.

Ella ducked into the girls' bathroom to hide until just before the bell rang. She didn't want to see Steph or Jane right now.

A girl she vaguely recognized was smoking out the bathroom window. The girl looked Ella over, took a deep drag of her cigarette, and blew out a grey puff of smoke. She was dressed all in black: a short, flared skirt, cropped turtleneck, tights, and lug-soled boots. She looked Ella up and down, her mouth curling in what Ella was sure was distaste. Ella was instantly self-conscious of her worn-out sweater and shapeless old corduroy pants. Lucinda had taken away all but a few basic items of her wardrobe.

Ella quickly entered one of the stalls and locked the door. She sat down on the very edge of the seat and dropped her head into her hands. Her charm bracelet jangled softly. She'd managed to slip it off and hide it in the attic before Lucinda made her give it away, and now she tried to get some comfort from the fact that it was still hers. But it was next to impossible to feel even a drop of happiness. It was so unfair. Everything she'd once had was slipping from her grasp. Her family, a place to call home, friends.

If her grades continued to fall, she was going to fail more than one class. Good-bye college. Good-bye future. And forget losing her troubles for an evening at the big-deal bash everyone else was going to—Staci and Drew included. They'd been in every store in the state, trying on dress after dress. But Ella hadn't even bothered to ask if she could go, too. Lucinda would make sure it was impossible.

Ella felt a wave of envy for all the other girls in town. She had to admit it to herself. She wanted nothing more than to go to that party. Plan her outfit. Dream about the guy she'd flirt with. Feel like a normal high-school girl again. Just for that one night.

She imagined herself gliding down the stairs of her house in some fabulous concoction, sailing out her front door, as Lucinda and company looked on. No asking for permission. No telling her plans to Lucinda beforehand. She'd just walk out the door when the time came.

And what could her stepmother do? She'd already taken away Ella's room, her clothes . . . and most of all, her dignity. Would she pile on more housework? It wasn't possible. Ella was doing as much as she could already. There wasn't anything left to take away. Ella felt her desires gathering momentum.

But wait. She'd thought she had nothing left to lose when she'd given away her father's clothes. And Lucinda had managed to figure out a way to punish her. So what would she resort to if Ella followed this one little daydream? Would Lucinda order her out of the house altogether?

It had been the one thing keeping Ella under her stepmother's thumb—the fear of losing the roof over her head and the home she had always known. But even that didn't feel like such a threat anymore. The house was hardly a place where Ella wanted to be. There were always chores to be done during every waking hour, and only the night brought the solace of her little attic hideaway that held mementos of the life she and her family had shared.

So what would it mean if Lucinda ordered her out? It was frightening not to know where she might sleep at night, but Ella wasn't sure she wouldn't be better off almost anywhere that was far away from Lucinda. Besides, Lucinda had a good a deal with Ella under her roof. Why would she give up a free pair of hard-working hands? No, Lucinda probably wouldn't throw her out—even if she went to the prince's party like every other girl.

Ella gave in to the delicious nervousness she had always felt before a big date or a special night out. Her heart beat a little too fast. She had butterflies in her stomach.

Oh, but what would she wear? She stared down at her balding corduroys and her old tennis shoes. It was bad enough coming to school in those clothes. Some days she just wanted to hide in the attic and—

Of course! The attic! And the trunk with her mother's old clothing—the crushed-velvet floor-length dresses and the wide-legged pants, the fringed vests and the beaded jackets—the Woodstock look was back in style. Ella wondered if she could find those wild shoes her mother used to have—the backless mules that were as shiny and clear as glass. She remembered playing dress-up in them when she was a little girl, and they'd been way too large for her child-sized feet. Let her stepsisters comb every store for something that special. You wouldn't find another pair of shoes like that anywhere.

Oh, it was going to be the best night! Ella stood up and raced out of the bathroom. She wasn't going to miss the prince's party! She half-ran back toward the lockers, dodging the kids in the crowded halls. Maybe she could still catch Steph and Jane before the bell and tell them she was going to the party, too.

Ten

"What are *you* so happy about?" Drew asked meanly.

Ella dusted the wooden frame of the recliner on which Drew was lounging, careful not to brush her arm with the dust rag. "No reason. Can't a person just be happy?" she answered, and went back to whistling to herself.

It was all planned. Steph and Jane were going to come by and pick Ella up later that evening. Steph had promised to French-braid her hair and weave in a glittery ribbon that would pick up the shine of the glass shoes. Jane was lending her a pair of long silver filigree earrings that would go perfectly with her vintage outfit and silver charm bracelet.

"Oh, by the way, Ella, I'm going to need my pink silk shirt washed before the party," Drew announced. "It's got to be done by hand."

Ella dusted the mantel over the fireplace, swiping at the framed photos of her stepsisters and stepmother. She interrupted her whistling long enough to say, "Sure, Drew."

"And I need the hem of my dress fixed," Staci said, coming into the living room just in time to hear her sister bossing Ella around. "The black one with the plunging neckline," Staci added.

"Plunging into nothing," Drew snickered.

"Oh, shut up," Staci retorted. "Just because you ooze out of everything in your closet—"

"I'm sure you'll both look fine," Ella said mildly.

Staci gave her a long look. "What's with her?" she asked her sister.

"How should I know?" Drew said crossly.

Ella gave one last wipe and headed out of the room, leaving Staci and Drew to pick on each other.

It was exactly the way she'd pictured it. Ella swept down the staircase, her mother's deep purple crushed-velvet skirt softly brushing the floor behind her. Her vest sparkled with dozens of sequin-sized mirrors, and a silky dark green shawl was draped around her shoulders. Her glass shoes made a satisfying click on the polished wooden stairs.

Drew and Staci were just getting ready to go to the prince's party. They were gelled and polished and styled to the hilt. Ella was overwhelmed by the smell of their perfume, mixing with their mother's smoke. Lucinda hovered over them, smoothing skirts and adjusting scarves, making sure every hair was in place for Prince William to see. All three of them looked up at Ella as she floated downstairs.

One of them let out a gasp. Ella wasn't sure which one.

"And where do you think you're going?" Lucinda asked.

Ella kept her composure. "To the prince's party."

"Mother!" Staci protested, looking at her to see what she would do.

"I think she's serious," Drew put in.

"Oh, but of course she isn't," Lucinda said calmly. She let out a snake of smoke. "She knows she isn't going anywhere until the house is properly cleaned."

Ella reached the bottom of the staircase. "But it is, Lucinda. I cleaned every inch of it just today."

Lucinda frowned. "I see. But you still have to mop this floor."

"Done," Ella said, trying to remain in control. "I finished it a few hours ago."

Lucinda's face was white with anger. "But it's dirty," she said. She took a long, furious drag on her cigarette and flicked the ash right onto the black-and-white tile floor.

Ella's stomach clenched. She dropped to the ground and brushed Lucinda's ash into the palm of her hand. She felt her shawl slip off.

"And there's another spot here," Lucinda said, flicking her cigarette again.

"Oh, Lucinda, please don't do this!" Ella pleaded.

"And right here." This time Lucinda threw down the butt and ground it out with her pointy-toed shoe. "Take a look." Suddenly she was grabbing Ella by the collar of her delicate, lace-trimmed, crushed-velvet dress.

Ella heard a dreadful rip as her stepmother thrust her toward the smashed cigarette butt. She fell down on the floor, her shoes flying off, her shawl half off and her dress slipping down one shoulder where the neck had been torn open. Her hopes and plans for the evening were coming apart just as quickly.

"Why, Lucinda? What pleasure can you get by denying me this one night?"

"I suggest you start mopping," Lucinda said chillingly, pointing to the ashes all over the floor now.

Out in front of the house, someone was honking. Steph. "Oh, please let me go. I'll have this floor cleaned up in no time, I promise," Ella pleaded.

Lucinda pulled open the front door and peered out into the purple dusk. Then she turned toward her daughters. "You two don't want to arrive too late. The prince is waiting. And on your way out, tell Ella's little friend that Ella isn't going to make it. And to get lost before I decide she's trespassing."

"No!" Ella cried. "No, tell her to wait!"

"I mean it," Lucinda said. "I'll go right to the phone and inform the police that there's someone on my property who hasn't been invited. Don't test me, Ella. You know I'll do it."

Ella felt the desperation washing over her.

"You wouldn't want your friend to spend the night in a holding cell when she could be at the party, do you? I don't think she'd be very pleased with you if that happened."

Drew and Staci smirked.

"Oh, okay, tell her to go without me," Ella said to them. "I'll catch up with her later."

"Sure you will," Staci said.

"Have fun, Ella," Drew said.

"We'll be thinking of you," Staci added as they sailed out the door. "Not."

Ella's anger surged with her tears. In her bare feet, she raced into the kitchen, grabbed a mop from the broom closet, and hastily filled a bucket of soapy water. She felt it slosh over her leg and onto the floor as she hauled it out to the foyer and set to work mopping the tiles furiously. Lucinda watched her stonily.

"There, it's clean again," Ella said desperately. "So I'll be going now—"

"Like that?" Lucinda asked with a laugh.

Ella looked down at herself. Her plush, flowing dress was torn and covered with soapy water. And where were her shoes? Over there, near the door. She moved to get them, but Lucinda picked them up first.

"Interesting looking," Lucinda said, holding the pretty shoes up for inspection. "Wherever did you get them? I thought we agreed you could only keep one pair of shoes." She hurled the glass shoes at Ella's feet. Ella jumped aside as one of the heels shattered against the hard floor, shards of glass shooting out like glittery arrows.

"You can clean that mess up, too!" Lucinda

ordered. Then she disappeared up the stairs.

Ella stared at the broken shoe, and her vision went blurry with tears. It was no use. No use at all to try for even one night of happiness. She was going to be mopping Lucinda's floors forever.

Forever? She touched the shoe that was still in one piece. Her mother's shoe. What would her mother have felt about her daughter just giving up? Ella heard a soft voice in her head. "Get up," it said. "Stand tall." Her own thoughts. Surely it must have been her own thoughts.

A bit unsteadily, Ella got to her feet. Well, perhaps she'd have to get a job before she could put herself through college. It would be harder and it would take longer than it might have if circumstances had been different. But it was possible. Of course it was. Sue Paulson's mother had put herself through school and raised two children. People did it all the time.

Ella couldn't go around feeling so sorry for herself. There was always hope as long as you looked for it. Yes. For a dizzying moment, she imagined she could actually see that spark of hope. Right in front of her—shimmering in the air like heat rising off the road at the height of summer.

Ella rubbed her eyes. They were playing tricks on her. It was all the stress, the exhaustion. She was seeing things. But there it was—a peculiar flickering, deepening into a ghostlike shadow.

"What's going on?" Ella only dared to whisper. The shadow glittered and quivered and seemed to take on depth. There was something there. But what?

Ella's breath caught in her throat. The shimmer of hope was taking on a human form. . . .

Ella squeezed her eyes closed. This wasn't happening—couldn't be happening. She opened them again and gasped. Standing before her was the woman who came around collecting for the needy.

"Hello, dear," she said gently.

"How—how did you get in here?" Ella stammered.

The woman shook her head. "Never mind me. You look like you could use some help. And that's what I do. I help people."

Ella knew she was staring. A tremor of amazement went through her. "Who are you?" she whispered.

The woman smiled. "You can call me Fay. We never did tell each other our names, did we?"

Ella found herself shaking her head. "I'm— Ella," she managed, even as she stood in disbelief.

"Ella. Pretty name. Very pretty young woman.

But look at those tears," Fay said, touching Ella's sad cheeks. "Come, let's dry them." She shook her hand, and out of midair, out of absolutely nothing, she held out a crisp, cotton handkerchief and offered it to Ella. "Here, dear."

Ella giggled—part nerves, part pure delight, like a child at a magic show. "How did you do that? Did you have it up your sleeve?" She took the handkerchief and dabbed at the corners of her eyes.

"Well, I think we all find we can pull so many things out of our sleeves when we really need to," Fay said. "Now what was it you were crying about, child?"

Ella handed the handkerchief back to Fay. Was she saying she *had* pulled it out of her sleeve? Fay folded it in half, then in half again, and put it back in one of the roomy pockets of her faded coat. Though she was a stranger, Ella felt comforted by Fay's presence.

"I was crying because I couldn't see any way out of this nightmare," Ella confided in her. "They're so cruel to me here. They treat me like I'm less than nothing. And I guess I've started to feel that maybe I am. That maybe there's no hope for me. . . ."

Fay took one of Ella's hands in both of her

own. "If you didn't have hope, I wouldn't be here." She gave a little laugh.

Ella thought about her glimmer of hope—and how she could swear she'd seen Fay materialize right out of it. Wonderment filled her all over again. How had Fay done that?

"So you *were* hopeful," Fay prodded.

"Well, yeah. I guess I did decide there was some hope. I mean, I won't be here forever," Ella answered. "And I'm just missing this one dumb party. . . ." But she felt her spirits tumble. "Just a party," she repeated flatly.

"Hmm. I see," Fay said. "And what's to stop you from going to this party?"

Ella looked up the stairs, not saying a word.

"You know, I have a strong hunch she's going to be very involved in a new horror novel. I doubt she'll be leaving her room tonight. And even if she did . . ."

Ella sighed. "She made sure the only outfit I could wear was totally ruined."

Fay studied her carefully. "Maybe not ruined. Maybe—well, for starters, your dress needs to be cleaned." Ella felt a funny, tingling sensation, as if she'd been plunged in a peppermint bath. She looked down at the long skirt, and the soapy stains had vanished.

"Oh, my—"

"Shh." Fay shook her head before Ella had a chance to speak another word. "You know the expression, never look a gift horse in the mouth? Now, let's see what we can do about that rip near the neck. There. Just a little mending." Ella could feel it coming back together as if someone were pulling up an invisible zipper. "And your shoes. What wonderful shoes. . . ." Fay passed a hand over the broken glass, and the shoes were both perfect again. She handed them to Ella. "And you wanted a special pair of earrings, something a little fancy for your hair? I think maybe just a tiny, slender braid on one side, with the rest of it flowing loose. Yes, and we'll weave in a silver ribbon."

Ella put a hand up and felt the delicate, dangling earrings. She gave a little gasp.

Fay looked her over. "Lovely. Oh, but let's touch up your makeup a bit. Your crying didn't help. Come, now, aren't you going to put those shoes on?"

Ella slipped her feet into her shoes as she gave her head a hard shake. This was impossible. Couldn't be happening. Then she let out a laugh— a big belly laugh—and it felt so good.

Fay touched Ella's shoulder and put a finger to her lips, pointing upstairs. "Shh."

"Oops!" Ella said, and she laughed some more.

Then Fay handed Ella's shawl to her, took her hand, and led her outside, closing the door softly behind them.

Dusk had settled into night, and a sprinkling of stars dotted the sky. The air was mild and sweet. Ella took a deep breath and felt light with freedom. This wasn't real. This *couldn't* be real. But it *was* happening. Somehow. Ella was out of the house and on her way to the prince's party.

Oh, but how was she going to get there? Steph would have picked up Jane by now, and they were probably at The Overlook already, searching the crowd to see who they knew. Feeling the music enter their bodies. Savoring the excitement of the night ahead.

"I suppose I could ride my bicycle," Ella said hesitantly. She took a few steps toward the old blue three-speed she rode to school. She wasn't sure she could manage in her fancy clothes—especially her delicate shoes. And The Overlook was on the other side of town, up a high, steep hill. She looked at Fay's rusty van, parked in the driveway. So she *had* driven here, though Ella hadn't heard her pull up. But then how had she gotten inside? And what about Ella's clothes? And her glass shoes?

"You know, my dear, I'd be happy to take you to the party myself," Fay said. "But you look so very beautiful, it would be a shame for you to arrive in my old wreck." She laughed. "And I'm not sure my clunker would make it all the way up that hill."

Ella watched Fay's gaze go toward her bicycle, leaning against the house under the night lights. And in the blink of an eye a little sports car suddenly appeared in its place, the same midnight blue as her bike.

"You do know how to drive, don't you, dear?" Fay asked.

Ella nodded, her pulse beating crazily. Her father had taught her to drive over the summer, and she'd passed her road test just before school had started. Fay reached into her coat pocket and pulled out a set of keys. She put them in Ella's hand.

"But how . . . I just—I'm not sure—I mean . . . I don't know what to say," Ella breathed.

"Don't say anything, dear. Just get going, yes? It's getting late already, and you don't want to miss another minute of what's ahead." She gave Ella a little push toward the car. "And by the way, this *is* real."

Ella wasn't quite sure how she got behind the

wheel. She felt absolutely giddy. Somehow she found the lights and started the car.

"Drive carefully," Fay said. "Oh, my dear—one thing. You must be home by midnight. By midnight, and not a moment later. It's the one thing I ask of you. There's a limit even to what's up my sleeve. . . ."

"Midnight," Ella repeated. "Yes. Yes, that's fine. Oh, thank you. However you did this. Thank you a million, zillion times!"

"Go, child," Fay told her. "And have the most wonderful time. . . ."

Eleven

Will snapped his fingers and spun around to the music. The driving bass line pulsed through the floor and into the thick soles of his shoes.

"Great party!" The pert honey-blonde he was dancing with had to yell to make herself heard above the loud music. Her dress shimmered blue and then violet and then red, as the room was bathed in changing color from the light show. The dance floor was packed with couples. Others watched from seats at round linen-draped tables, their plates heaped with food from the buffet table.

"Glad you're enjoying yourself—" Julie? Jenny? Will's head reeled with names and faces and voices.

Will must have danced with every available girl in the state of Connecticut already—maybe every girl in all of New England—and the party had only started about an hour ago. He'd wind down with one girl, and before he'd taken his next breath, he was spinning around the floor with someone else. Short and tall, pretty and homely, good dancers and bad ones—they were all over him, like flies to honey.

The band wailed out the last notes of the song. "Well, thanks for the dance. It was a pleasure to meet you," Will said to Julie-Jenny, in proper princely fashion.

"Prince Will!" said a voice at his side, even before Julie-Jenny had begun to make her way off the dance floor. Will vaguely recognized a tall, gangly girl from school. She had a group of friends with her, all eyes on him. For a split second, Will was flattered. But he couldn't fool himself. He wished he could believe it was because of his magnetic personality, or because he had an overwhelming sex appeal.

Yeah, right, Will, he told himself. But most of the girls he'd danced with this evening were barely acquainted with him, or had been introduced to him for the first time tonight. All they knew was that he was a prince—a real, live prince. And all he knew was that someone had let it out of the bag that he was searching for a princess.

Someone. He knew exactly who that someone

was as he'd spotted Chris holding court by the buffet table, surrounded by a group of pretty partygoers. According to one girl Will had danced with, Chris had appointed himself Will's social coordinator. Chris had promised introductions and that he'd put in a good word to His Willness for anyone he deemed lovely enough. A one-man selection committee who was, no doubt, stuffing his little black book full of new names and telephone numbers.

And where was Trish, the girl Chris had been practically drooling over for weeks? Will was going to have to have a talk with Chris later. Or maybe he'd just leave him to the mercy of the male guests at the party, several of whom he could see casting dirty looks at Chris as they'd piled food on their plates.

Kenny, nursing a cup of punch in a corner of the room, didn't look too happy, either. Will saw him glance over at Chris with a mixture of envy and annoyance on his face. Will made a mental note to introduce Kenny to some of the nicer girls he'd met. After he got a little break from this scene.

Will made a beeline for the door of The Overlook. He needed some air and a few moments of quiet. A look at the stars and a chance to recharge.

But he ran right into a girl blocking his exit. "Oh, man, I'm sorry," he said. Even looking the other way, he wondered how he could have missed the overpowering smell of her perfume. He stifled a cough. This girl spilled out of her blouse and short, tight leather skirt. He wasn't certain, but he thought he'd seen her around school.

"You can bump into me any time you want, Your Highness," she answered flirtatiously. She teetered forward in absurdly high heels and put a hand on his forearm. Her long red nails looked like weapons. "You're not leaving your own party, are you?"

Will felt his cheeks coloring with embarrassment. "I was stepping outside for some fresh air. Just for a moment. I wasn't really leaving . . ."

"Oh, that sounds perfect," the girl gushed. "I could use a breather, too." She turned, as if to accompany Will outside.

Trapped. Will saw his escape hatch closing up. "I, um, ah—oh, hey, I love this song! Would you like to dance?" he quickly improvised as the band went into a cover of an old Stevie Wonder tune. He barely waited for an answer before steering the girl out onto the floor. By the middle of the song, he'd maneuvered them all the way across the room and over toward the buffet table. By the end of the song, he'd gotten Chris's attention and motioned him over. He saw Chris's eyebrows go up as he tore himself away from his little crowd of admirers.

"Chris, I want you to meet a new friend of mine," he said, in the lull between songs. "This is—" He hadn't even asked her name.

"Drew," the girl said, misreading his attentions and leaning in close to Will.

Will turned his head and tried not to breathe in her perfume. "Drew, this is Chris," he said. "I think you two might really get along. Why don't you dance this next dance together?"

"But . . ." they both sputtered.

But before either one of them had a chance to protest any further, Will took off, working his way back through the crowded room, and not letting anyone stop him on his way to the exit.

Will stepped into the night and closed the door behind him. A quiet calm descended on him like a soft, light snow. The music faded into a muted sound. The air was cool and fresh. Will took a deep breath and felt himself relax. Not a princely way to behave toward his best friend or that girl, but he just had to have a few moments alone.

He followed the narrow slate path around the side of the restaurant, to where the lawn ended in a thick, low stone wall, behind which the earth dropped off in a rocky cliff. The lights of town glittered below like reflections of stars. A bright half-moon illuminated the rolling foothills at the edge of town that gave way to mountains in the distance.

Will stared out into the peaceful night. He knew any minute now, his bodyguard would be easing his bulky frame through the crowded restaurant, trying to find out where Will had gotten to. He didn't care. He just needed a little time alone to shake off the feeling of being the prized piece at an auction.

Sophie Bonnard from school had told him she'd even heard a rumor that he was going to choose a bride at the end of the night—as if the female guests were participants in some sort of absurd lottery. Will shook his head. He'd been looking forward to this party, too.

On the far side of the lawn, he heard a car pulling into the crowded Overlook parking lot. He watched indifferently as the driver circled around, searching for an empty spot. Nice little blue sports car. It finally came to a stop in a puddle of light from a lamppost, so Will could easily see the car door opening and a girl getting out.

A princess wannabee in a fancy car, Will

thought to himself, but at the same time, he noticed her graceful bearing and the fluid way she moved her tall, slender body. She shut her car door and looked around—tentatively, it seemed to Will. She took a few steps, hugging a shawl around her against the coolness of the evening, and then stopped to look up at the stars. Will smiled.

The girl began walking across the lawn, getting nearer to where Will stood. He watched her and as she drew close enough for him to see her face, he couldn't believe his eyes. This girl was so lovely. Her outfit shimmered and shone like stardust, but it was her easy elegance and natural beauty that held Will's attention. He realized he was staring.

"Hello," he called out to her.

"Hi," she answered softly, meeting him where he stood. "Isn't the sky incredible tonight?"

He nodded. He wanted to say, "*You're* incredible."

"It's such a treat to be able to have a few quiet moments to look at it." She gave a little laugh. "Maybe that sounds corny to you."

"No. I know exactly what you mean," Will said. And he did. "It's so much bigger than any personal problem. It kind of puts things in perspective, doesn't it?"

"You mean, like there are more possibilities

than you realize?" the girl asked. "That you're not as—I don't know—closed in, maybe, as you think?"

Will had a strange feeling that this girl truly understood how he felt. Perhaps she, too, was searching for some opening in a future that had her locked in tight. The moonlight seemed to shine in her almond-shaped eyes. Who was she, this beautiful, sensitive girl who seemed to give voice to Will's very own thoughts?

"I don't believe we've had the pleasure of meeting before," he said. "You are—?"

The girl suddenly looked uncomfortable. She dropped her gaze to the grassy ground. "I'm—nobody," she whispered.

Will felt an electric thrill. "Wow, I can't believe it. I totally understand what you're saying. There are plenty of times I'd just like to forget about who I am, too."

The girl raised her eyes to meet his. "You would?"

Will nodded. "So if you want to be nobody tonight, it's okay with me."

But his heart knew better. It was telling him that, far from being nobody, this was the girl he'd been dreaming about.

Twelve

Ella was grateful that the boy didn't push to find out who she was. Tonight, she didn't want to be Ella Browning, chief floor scrubber and attic dweller. She'd come here to be a regular girl—part of the crowd, soaking up the music and the fun. But as she looked into this handsome boy's eyes, the desire to throw herself into the crowd faded away. She was happy just standing here, talking to him about the night sky. She felt instantly comfortable with him. Maybe it was part of the whole magic of the evening. And he even looked familiar.

"You know, I think I've seen you somewhere before," she said.

A funny expression passed across the boy's face. Ella couldn't quite read it. He was silent for a few moments. Had she said something wrong?

But then he smiled again—a warm smile that went up more at one corner of his mouth than the other. "Maybe you've seen me in town or something," he said. "But how about if we say that tonight I'm a nobody, too? Two nobodies."

Ella felt a welcome ripple of recognition. This boy was like her! He, too, wanted a night to forget about whatever burdens he was carrying. He understood her, didn't he? He seemed to know just how she was feeling, and just how to show her that it was okay.

The faint strains of a slow, romantic song floated out of the restaurant. "Would you like to dance?" the boy asked her.

Ella felt a tickle of shyness, but she wanted to dance with him very much. She nodded. "I'd like that." And then the boy was holding her in his arms and they were swaying to the music.

Ella was dizzy with the mild scent of his shampoo, and gentle strength of his body pressed to hers, the glittering of the stars overhead, and the pungent coolness of the air.

This has to be another one of Fay's perfect spells, Ella thought. Spells that couldn't possibly be real. Except that Ella was here. And in the arms of a wonderful guy, on their own private, grassy dance floor, under a perfect sky. Ella was more convinced than ever that this whole evening had to turned out to be one marvelous dream.

*   *   *

Ella wasn't sure how much time had passed. They'd danced. They'd talked. They liked the same songs that escaped the restaurant to hover quietly on the air.

He'd told her all about his travels on his computer, making them sound as exciting as any real trip. He'd pointed out the constellations—together they could name all of them. They'd danced some more.

Now they glided and spun slowly, their bodies moving in unison, deliciously aware of each other. The music faded to the faintest back beat as they danced toward the stone wall at the edge of the property. Coming to a gradual stop, they released each other only hesitantly.

"I love being in the mountains like this," the boy said, as they gazed out at the dark silhouettes of the peaks and valleys. "It makes you feel like nature and the world around you is so powerful, you know? Like it's so much bigger than any individual thing. Sort of puts things in perspective."

Ella nodded. "Yeah, but at the same time, I feel kind of nestled in by them. I don't know. Maybe it's because I grew up hiking and cross-country skiing and stuff right here in these mountains. See that pointy peak on the left?" She indicated with her hand. "There's this one really beautiful trail that twists and turns and winds all the way from the base to the top. It's my favorite."

They stood side by side, not touching, yet feeling each other's nearness. "I love taking long walks in the woods," the boy said. "Maybe you could show me that trail sometime."

Ella felt a current of happiness. Overhead, the Big Dipper poured out its starry magic on them.

Back by The Overlook, a few guests had begun to leave the party. A trio headed for the parking lot, the sound of their laughter trailing behind them.

"Looks like things are slowing down in there," Ella commented. "Do you think we should go inside?"

The boy shrugged. "Why?"

Ella laughed. "I don't know. Before the party's over. I mean, that's why we both came tonight, right? And then maybe we could meet the prince."

Now it was the boy's turn to laugh. "Hey, if you've seen one prince, you've seen them all."

"You mean you're not curious about him? A real prince? An actual prince in our little town? Did you ever read that play *A Connecticut Yankee in King Arthur's Court*? Where that guy time-travels from New England to King Arthur's England? Well, I guess this is sort of the opposite.

You know, *A Prince of the Royal Court in Yankee Connecticut*."

The boy laughed again. "Yeah, I liked that play too. But the prince?" He let out a sigh. "He's just a figurehead. Someone to photograph, someone to gossip about in the newspapers. I mean, face it—a prince in this day and age? It's the politicians who have the real power, who make the real decisions. The presidents, the prime ministers—the ones the people elect. The prince? He's just a party boy."

Ella was surprised at the hard edge in his voice. Maybe he was envious of someone who had everything he could possibly want. Ella could certainly understand that. There was so much in life she longed for these days. The boy must feel the same way. Yet the thought of being a prince—a genuine prince—struck her as terribly romantic. Something from the pages of a storybook that had somehow found its way into real life. Something magical. Like this magical night. Ella was hit with another wave of amazement. But she was afraid to think too hard about how this had all happened, for fear that her good fortune would dissolve into dismal reality.

But the prince—well, he was real. "I don't know," she said to the boy. "Politicians have to answer to public opinion, and the public looks to its important people—the people you read about, for guidance. Their opinions and what they do can really make a difference."

"You think?"

"Well, sure. I mean, look. If someone famous lends their name to something, say, just for example, that the prince set up some sort of foundation to help people who were down on their luck—really down—no roof over their heads, no decent clothes or food . . ." Ella thought about the men and women for whom Fay took up her annual collection. Magical, bighearted Fay. "You can bet that if the prince was involved, it would get plenty of notice and support, right?"

The boy smiled. "Well, yeah . . ."

"And so the elected officials would have to start paying attention, too. The rain forest, world hunger, AIDS—there are rock stars and movie stars and princesses and all kinds of famous people who are helping make us more aware of the most important issues. Prince Will could do that too. I mean, unless you happen to know that he *is* only interested in partying. . . ."

The boy shook his head. "No. No, I didn't mean to suggest that at all. You know, you're a very special person. . . ." He turned to look at her, their faces only inches apart.

Ella felt them drawing together, his palm gently caressing her cheek, her hands on his shoulders as she gazed up at him. And then their lips found each other, and they were joined in the sweetest, deepest kiss. Ella's body tingled. No kiss had ever felt this way before. The faint music surrounded them. Down in the valley, the church bells were ringing out—

Oh, no! No—the church bells were ringing midnight! Ella pulled back suddenly. The tingling! It was exactly the way she'd felt when Fay had worked her magic back at the house. That peppermint tingle. Midnight. Fay had warned her to be home by midnight, and not a minute later.

I can't leave now. Ella longed to stay with this boy with all her heart and soul. *What can happen to me anyway?* she thought. *I'm not going to turn into a toad or something.* But she couldn't deny the powerful, dreamlike magic at work tonight. This was a night when anything could happen.

Ella forced herself to start across the grass, calling out a good-bye over her shoulder. "I've had the most wonderful evening—the best night of my life," she told the boy. "But I have to go . . ." The tingling was getting stronger.

"Wait! Please!" he called after her. "I don't

even know your name. I thought you wanted to meet the prince. . . ."

But Ella had already reached the edge of the parking lot and was running toward the little blue sports car. Frantically, she felt around for the key in the deep inside pocket of her vest. The church bells continued their round, slow chiming. Ella moved faster. She felt one glass slipper fly off her foot, but there was no time to stop and pick it up.

As she jumped behind the wheel of the car and started the ignition, she saw the boy coming after her. How she wanted to wait for him. But Fay's words echoed in her mind, and the peppermint tingle raced through her body. She put the car in gear, floored the gas pedal, and took off with a squeal of tires. As the last stroke of twelve rose from town, she pulled around a sharp bend in the road.

And suddenly she was struggling to keep her balance on her old bicycle. A shiver of shock went through her. As she gained her equilibrium on the two-wheeler, she realized that her shawl had slipped off behind her somewhere, and that one shoulder was bare to the night where her dress was torn again. She didn't even have to look to know that the long skirt was covered with soap stains or that her hair and face were a mess. The party was over. The dream had vanished. And Ella had a long, cold ride home, one glass slipper and one bare foot on the worn rubber pedals of her bike.

But the wonder of the evening was enough to make her feel warm. How had it happened? She couldn't say. It was as mysterious and magical as falling in love. Yes, falling in love—if only for one perfect night. . . .

Thirteen

"You've been moping over that thing all morning," Chris said to Will, poking him in his side.

Will sat on his bed and stared at the delicate crystal shoe—its slender, curved heel, its open back, its gently pointed toe. He watched the way it gleamed with every color of the rainbow as it caught the light coming through his window.

"Yeah, Will, come on," Kenny said. Even he couldn't seem to understand. "It's just a shoe. Okay, an unusual shoe. I mean, in fact, I've never seen a shoe like it before. . . ."

"Yo, Kenny, cool it!" Chris ordered. "You want to encourage him, or something?"

"You guys just don't get it," Will said. "I look at this shoe, and I see her. The way she walked, the way she danced, the outline of her legs under that long velvet dress, her face, her voice. . . . She was so graceful and elegant—but not at all stuck-up. I mean, I can feel her whole spirit in that shoe."

"Uh-oh, watch out," Chris sang in a flaky voice. "It looks like Will has gone New Age on us."

Will stopped looking at the shoe long enough to shoot Chris a dirty look. "Do you think you can get off my case for a few minutes?"

"Who, me? Hey, that party was *my* idea. I practically arranged the whole thing for you. And the only thanks I got was when you tried to set me up with some cow marinated in Chanel number five." Without getting out of his chair, Chris leaned down, grabbed the Nerf basketball lying on the carpet, and took an angry, wild shot at the basket on the back of Will's door.

"Air ball," Kenny commented.

Chris frowned, but Will saw that it was directed at him, not at Kenny. "Look, Chris, everyone at that party seemed to have the idea that there was going to be a new princess-to-be at the end of the night—and that you were the man with the prince's ear. Made you pretty popular with the girls, didn't it?"

"I was only doing it for you. So you wouldn't have to spend your Christmas vacation with Edith whose-a-ma-Dussel. Christmas vacation and the rest of your life."

"Edith *Highsmith*. *Elsa* Von Dussel." The thought of escorting snobby Edith and ugly Elsa to all those holiday parties made Will ache even more for his mystery girl.

"Whoever," Chris said. "You know I was just trying to do you a favor—screening the girls for you."

Will rolled his eyes. "Yeah, well, that one I made you dance with fell through the cracks, didn't she?"

"Her? She couldn't fall through an opening the size of a barn door," Chris shot back.

"And why weren't you with Trish, anyway?" Will asked.

Chris looked chagrined. He took a moment to answer. "She said I was paying too much attention to all those other girls. So maybe I deserved to dance with that Drew person. Anyway, we weren't talking about me," he added, getting off that fiery subject before he really felt the burn. "We were talking about you. And, hey, my plan worked, didn't it? You *did* meet someone who made your royal heart go pitter-patter."

Will closed his eyes. He could feel the softness of her face, see the shine of her long brown hair in the moonlight. "Yeah, I did. For all the good it's going to do me when I don't even know her name." He opened his eyes and looked at Chris. "And if your intention really was to help me get together with her, you could at least be a little more sympathetic. I mean, what if *you'd* met the girl of your dreams, and you only had one evening to spend with her?" Will turned to Kenny. He might be easier to reach. "C'mon, Kenny, how do you think *you'd* feel?"

Kenny arched an eyebrow. "How could I have met the girl of my dreams? Between the ones running after you, and the ones flocking around Chris, there weren't too many others left for me to meet. I mean, even if I *had* worked up the nerve to ask any of them to dance."

Will felt bad. While he'd been dancing under the stars with an incredible girl, Kenny had only been dreaming about it. "Hey, it'll happen to you one day."

Kenny shrugged doubtfully.

"You just need to get over your shyness. Give those girls a chance to get to know you. And when you do—well, I hope she won't disappear on you just as you realize you're falling in love." Will swallowed hard. "There. I said it. I think I fell in love with her. I *know* I did."

"But, Will," Chris began, "you were with her only for a few hours."

Will felt a sting of annoyance. "That's more time than *you* spend getting to know a girl."

"Peace, you guys. I think what Chris really means is that we don't want to see you get hurt," Kenny said diplomatically. "You don't know anything about this girl. I mean, for starters, why wouldn't she even tell you her name?"

"Maybe for the same reason I didn't tell her mine. Because I wanted to be myself for a little while—not some title or position."

"You mean, you think she's a princess or something?" Kenny said doubtfully.

"Maybe 'or something.' I don't know. Could be her parents are rich and famous," Will said, thinking about her expensive little car. "And she didn't want me to get the wrong idea. Which I did for about a second or two. Or maybe her father's the new mayor."

"Will, the new mayor's a woman," Chris pointed out. "And her daughter's in elementary school. Kinda young for you, don't you think?"

"Oh. Well, I don't really care who the girl is, anyway. It doesn't matter. And I don't need to spend any more time with her to know how special she is. You guys just don't understand."

"Look, if that's true, you're one lucky guy," Kenny said, a note of envy in his voice. "And it's not that we're not with you all the way. Both of us. But, Will, you did tell us that this girl took off on you. Don't forget that."

Will wanted to shut his ears to his own worst thoughts. She suddenly decided she didn't like him. She didn't want to be kissed by him. She'd realized who he was, and was furious that he was holding back on her. But her words as she'd raced to her car—it had been the best evening of her life. No, there was some other reason she'd pulled a disappearing act. She'd seemed nervous about something. But about what? Should he be afraid for her? Will took her shoe in his hands, feeling its smooth weight.

"We wouldn't be your friends if we weren't a little worried about you," Chris said, softening a bit. "I mean, you've spent the whole day with a shoe. It's not—normal, Will."

Neither Chris nor Kenny could hold in a little laugh. Will joined in. "Okay, so I have a foot fetish." They laughed harder. But then Will grew serious again. "The thing is, it's all I have of her."

"Will, all we're saying is the shoe's not going to get you anywhere," Chris told him. "You can't clone your dream girl out of her shoe."

"Yeah, what are you going to do, Will?" Kenny asked.

Will shook his head slowly. "I don't know. I really don't know. But you guys are right. I have to do something. I have to find her. I just don't know how."

Ella went over every detail of her evening. And over and over. But she stopped short, each time, of the moment when the church bells had begun chiming midnight. She bustled around the kitchen preparing dinner, but in her mind she was dancing under the stars, feeling the easy sway of her body and his, the delicious weight of his arms around her, his scent, the soft, cool breeze. . . .

"Well, you really missed it, Ella." Drew's voice broke unpleasantly into Ella's memories. "It was the most incredible party."

"It was," Ella said dreamily. She narrowly missed her finger as she sliced mushrooms for a stir-fry. "I mean, it was?"

"Yeah, there was a live band and fresh flowers on every table, and this incredible spread—smoked salmon and these miniature vegetable pastries—and fresh strawberries and chocolate truffles, and—"

"And Drew sampled absolutely everything," Staci put in.

Drew shot her a look. "I was going to say how I danced with the prince. And you, little sister, are jealous."

Ella didn't pay much attention to her stepsisters fighting. She felt a tickle of curiosity about the party—the food, the way the restaurant had been decorated, who was there from school. She wondered who Steph had danced with, and whether she'd had fun. Maybe Ella *should* have gone inside. But no. It couldn't have gotten any better than it had been. Not even dancing with the prince himself would have been nicer than dancing with her handsome, wonderful boy.

"Hah!" Staci said harshly to her sister. "The prince danced with loads of girls. And may I remind you that as soon as he finished with you, he left his own party and spent the rest of the night outside with some other girl?"

Drew frowned. "Yeah, well . . . it was pretty rude of him, not even sticking around for his guests. . . ."

Ella couldn't contain a little laugh. "I guess he wanted to enjoy the nice weather. Chilly, but nice. "The stars were beautiful last night." So Prince William had been enjoying his party under the night sky, too. Ella felt an itch of curiosity about him. Too bad they hadn't met up with him outside the restaurant. They must have been out back, on the other side of The Overlook.

"Yeah, we could see him out there on the

lawn between the restaurant and the parking lot," Staci said. "Dancing all close and romantic with this girl."

Another couple dancing on the same stretch of lawn? There *hadn't* been any other couple. At least not while Ella was there. Suddenly she felt a tremor of shock. "Staci, what did you just say? The girl—do you know who she was?"

Staci shrugged. "She was tall and really graceful, and she had on some long, flowing outfit—you could almost see it glittering. But it was dark out there, and it was hard to get a really good look."

Ella had to keep from gasping. *Oh, no. The prince!* Was it possible? She had spent the entire evening with the prince! Her knife clattered to the counter. She felt dizzy. She'd danced with Prince William. She'd kissed Prince William! She thought about the sweet, moist softness of his lips. The prince! If that wasn't proof of a magic spell, what was?

Suddenly certain things they'd said to each other took on a whole new light. "There are plenty of times I'd like to forget about who I am, too," the boy had said. And the way she had stuck up for being a prince in this day and age—why, she'd been making her point to the prince himself! Ella felt her cheeks color over that. But the boy—Prince

Will—hadn't seemed to mind. Quite the opposite, Ella thought, reliving their kiss in her mind. His lips. The strong, gentle way he held her, his hands stroking her hair . . . *Oh, my gosh, the prince kissed me! I kissed Prince Will!*

Ella rode on a cloud of elation. Her mystery boy was the prince himself! No wonder he looked familiar. Ella almost laughed out loud. And he'd chosen to be with *her*, not any of his other guests. Not Drew or Staci or anyone else who'd been watching them out the big glass windows of The Overlook. Watching the prince. And watching *her*!

"So no one knew anything about the girl?" Ella couldn't keep herself from asking.

Staci shrugged. "I don't know. I thought there was something familiar about her."

"Yeah," Drew said, actually agreeing with her sister for once. "She must be someone famous. A movie star, or maybe she's royalty, too."

Ella felt a stab of discouragement. Is that what the prince had thought? That his nobody was really a somebody? Certainly Ella had been mistaken when she'd looked into his eyes and imagined a mirror to her very own situation. If he'd done the same, he'd be shocked if he found out that his nobody was exactly that.

"Okay, so he only danced with me once,"

Drew went on. "But only because that girl was, like, a perfect match for him."

Ella's mood tumbled lower. A perfect match? A girl with nothing and a boy with everything? The prince had danced with her. Yes. And talked with her and even kissed her. He'd told her she was special. But only because he didn't know who she truly was. Oh, it had seemed real enough—their feelings for each other, the good conversation, the specialness of their evening together. Ella had been certain they'd both felt it. But it was only part of Fay's magic spell. A spell that had dissolved at midnight. A prince in love with her, Ella Browning, who was nothing and nobody? Maybe. But only until the clock struck twelve and the magic had worn off.

Ella felt her romantic memories slipping from her grasp. Perhaps it would have been better never to find out who her prince was.

"Yo, man, you gonna take that shoe to practice with you?" Chris razzed Will. He and Kenny had stopped by to pick up Will on the way to a lacrosse scrimmage. They stood in his doorway, Kenny in sweats, Chris in baggy gym shorts with longer, Lycra shorts underneath. "You can put it front and center on the bleachers. Make some fancy moves. Score some points. Impress the heck out of that shoe."

Chris and Kenny both guffawed loudly. Will joined in the laughter, but more weakly. "Come on, guys. It's not that funny. I mean, that shoe's the only link I have with the girl I love, and I can't find a trace of her anywhere else. No blue sports car like hers registered to anyone in town—I had someone check for me down at Motor Vehicles. No one I've described her to has any idea who she could be."

"So she's not from around here," Kenny reasoned. "You said yourself you thought she was some big shot."

"Yeah, some exotic woman with a secret," Will said dreamily, picturing the stars reflected in her eyes, the moonlight shimmering off her dress and in her silky hair. He did remember her almost as some celestial creature, or at least someone who was heavenly sweet. But someone from far away?

"No, I'm sure she's from around here," he said to Kenny, thinking of the mountains she knew so well, and the trails she'd told him she'd been hiking all her life. "She knows this whole area as if it were her backyard. She grew up here. She practically said so herself. But that and her shoe are my only clues about her." Will pulled on his sweatpants and laced up his cleats.

"So you're going to obsess over a shoe?" Chris asked. "I mean, you can't very well bring the shoe home with you. Tell Patricia and Lady Von Jane that you're standing them up for a backless glass shoe."

Will gave a sour chuckle. "That's not the worst idea." He grabbed his keys from his desk. Casting a quick look at the shoe on his bed, he locked his door behind him, tossed his keys in his gym bag, and he and Chris and Kenny headed out.

"You could introduce the shoe to your parents," Kenny said, jumping in too. "She won't be much trouble. Doesn't eat anything, and she's never rude or loud."

Will laughed in spite of himself. "And she's a wonderful dancer—at least on the right foot. I mean the left foot. It's a left shoe, you know."

"I can just see you walking down the aisle with your precious shoe," Chris put in. "The guests will ooh and ahh. Look how beautiful she is. Look how she shines!"

The three boys walked out into the slightly overcast, chilly afternoon. "But seriously, Will," Kenny said.

Will bit his lip. When he finally spoke, it was to

echo his friend's word. "Seriously . . . Well, seriously, that shoe is the only tip I have about her. So I've been thinking that what I'm going to do next is to put something in the local paper. I'll say that one of my guests lost a shoe at my party, and I'd like the honor of returning it, continuing the friendship we began."

"You're going to beg for her in public?" Chris asked disapprovingly.

"I don't see it as begging," Will said, with a touch of annoyance. "I see it as the only possibility. And, hey, maybe if you did a little begging yourself, Tricia might realize she actually means something to you."

"Hey, guys, why don't you save it for the playing field," Kenny suggested mildly. "Maybe we can ask the coach to put you on opposite sides of the scrimmage. And don't forget that some of us aren't even lucky enough to have any girl problems."

"I'm sorry, Kenny," Will said sincerely. He paused. "But listen, anytime you want, I have a fabulous dress shoe you could borrow. . . ."

The boys' laughter rose like chimney smoke in the late fall air.

Fourteen

"Well, well! You're quite the tricky one, aren't you?" Lucinda filled the doorway to Ella's attic room, anger simmering under her mocking smile. "I don't know how you managed to do it, but you certainly pulled off a good one, didn't you?"

"What time is it?" Ella jumped out of her peaceful sleep. Even the most piercing alarm clock couldn't have been half as frightening as waking to the sound of Lucinda's booming voice. Only the weakest rays of daylight crept in through the high windows, and a translucent moon was still visible in the sky.

"I suppose now that you're practicing to be a famous lady of the court, you intend to sleep all day, too?" Lucinda snapped.

A lady of the court? Oh, no, Lucinda must have found out about the prince's party. Ella sat up in bed. "Surely, I don't know what you're talking about," she said nervously.

"'Surely, I don't know,'" Lucinda imitated in a high, honeyed voice. "You may look sweet and innocent, but I know better. And you know I know. So don't play coy with me." She tossed a copy of the *Courant* on the bed. Ella couldn't imagine how the town newspaper fit into this. "Page ten," her stepmother said.

Ella riffled through the pages, curiosity mixing with dread. With Lucinda paying a personal visit to the attic, Ella knew it couldn't be anything good. But as she opened to page ten, she got a delicious shock. There was a picture of her glass shoe, the one she'd left behind as she'd fled the prince's party. And the borders of the photo were trimmed in the shape of a heart! Ella had been carrying the other shoe around in her sweatshirt pocket, just feeling its weight and the strength of the memories it held.

She quickly read what was printed underneath the newspaper photo, and for a moment, she heard the faint strains of a slow, romantic old song she and Prince William had danced to, remembered the feel of his arms around her. He was searching for her! The boy—*the prince*—was trying to find her!

"I distinctly remember that shoe meeting with an unfortunate accident," Lucinda said. "Unless some other girl at the party just happened to have found and bought a pair of those exact same, highly unusual shoes . . ."

Some other girl. The music in Ella's head stopped abruptly. No, it hadn't been some other girl, but it might as well have been. The prince was certainly looking for his perfect match, as Drew had put it. Someone who mirrored his own dreams and desires. Not someone who was little more than a slave.

"But then maybe a very clever someone managed to put that shoe together somehow and sneak off right under my nose. If that's so, well, don't wait a moment longer to invite your prince to return it. No, you mustn't keep him waiting. I'm sure he'll be absolutely fascinated to see who his dream woman really is." Lucinda looked as if someone had just told her a hilarious joke.

"You can entertain him right here, in your little garret—I'm sure he's never seen anything quite like it." She made a point of looking around at the stacks of boxes, the clutter, the thin mattress on the floor, the bare windows. "And he'll be delighted, I'm sure, to hear how beautifully you wash and iron." She laughed meanly.

Ella felt a fat tear rolling down her cheek, as Lucinda spoke Ella's deepest fears out loud. "Why don't you just—leave me alone," Ella whispered.

Lucinda smiled. "Far be it from me not give my own stepdaughter what she wants." She turned on her spiked heel, and Ella could hear her stomping her way back downstairs.

Through blurry eyes, Ella stared at the black-and-white newsprint heart with the shoe inside it. *Try to savor the good memories,* she scolded herself, roughly wiping at her tears with the back of her hand. *Try to remember that for one night, one magical, perfect night, you were good enough for a prince.*

But the tears wouldn't stop, and Ella couldn't find pleasure in her night of memories. Because now she knew what she was missing. Now she knew how special a boy could make her feel, and she was consumed by emptiness because he was gone. She didn't care that he was a prince. No. He'd made her evening wonderful when he was a nobody—just like she was. But the magic was over. Now that she knew who he was, she couldn't expect him to feel the same way about her. Not if he ever found out who she really was. For once, Ella thought miserably, Lucinda was right.

*   *   *

Prince Will sat in a rear booth in the Acropolis Diner with Chris and Kenny. His back was to the crowd in the room, and he slouched in his seat. Today, in particular, he was in no mood for calling attention to himself. He hoped his bodyguard, parked outside the aluminum-sided diner in a fancy black car, wasn't too obvious. He kept his sunglasses on as he worked on his burger.

"Don't feel bad," Chris said, stealing a french fry off Will's plate. "There's always your lovely, well-behaved shoe."

Will didn't laugh. The shoe jokes had worn thin, and he was too unhappy to care. "She doesn't want to see me again. That's why she ran away. I should have been big enough to face the truth right then and there. . . ."

"Look, maybe she doesn't read the *Courant*," Kenny suggested consolingly. For such a nice guy, he sure could attack a plate of food viciously. Will watched as Kenny did a number on his burger de-luxe with a side of macaroni and cheese, and a jumbo chocolate shake.

"Forget the *Courant!*" Will hadn't been able to rustle up much interest in food since the night of his party. Nothing seemed to have much taste. He ate his burger out of hunger only. "What about all the cheap journalists who picked up the story and turned it into some kind of entertainment-of-the-week? 'Prince Wears Heart on Sleeve,'" Will quoted. "'Public Display of Affection.' 'She Loves Us, She Loves Us Not.' Pretty lame use of the royal 'we,' wouldn't you say? And that's just a few of them. But the point is, everyone from here to Timbuktu has heard about me by now. She must know I'm looking for her. Whoever she is," Will took a sip of ginger ale. "I mean, even my parents know. And, boy, am I in deep trouble," he added, a tightness in his chest.

"Yeah? Royal wrath?" Chris asked.

Will nodded. "'It's not dignified, son. It's not done. You must know better. You're making quite a fool of yourself, and us as well. You know the tabloids are having a field day. They're turning this into a major scandal. We're disappointed in you.' In other words, they're furious. They've even threatened to pull me out of Chason. Whisk me back to the palace, where they can keep an eye on me."

"And you won't graduate?" Kenny asked, pausing from his meal only long enough to form the question.

"Graduate?" Will raised his shoulders. "I wasn't even thinking about *that*. If they make me come home, I'll never find my shoe-girl. Who would have thought that dancing with someone I really liked could turn into such a scandal?"

"Will, far be it from me to spoil your romantic misery, but don't forget that there's a flip side to all this publicity," Chris commented. "I mean, the letters, the phone calls to school—and how about those girls trying to get into the dorm? They're literally trying to break down the door. All of them begging to tell you that glass shoe is theirs."

"Glass shoes must be a hot item these days," Kenny joked. "Even though no one had ever owned a pair before last week. Hard to keep up with these rapid fashion trends. But really, Chris is right, Will. Did you see this stack of mail I went through for you?" He patted a big pile on the table. "And that's just what the school received today. There's even one from some girl in France. A Parisian girl. She's pretty, too. Sent a photo along."

Chris reached for the pile. "Yeah? Give it to me. I'll answer it."

Kenny kept his hand over the pile of letters. "You're a lucky guy, Will."

Will wished he could feel lucky. But every night since his party, he'd found himself longing for the girl and everything about her, remembering every moment of their evening, every word they'd shared. And he lulled himself to sleep by imagining the two of them together again, hiking up one of her favorite trails, reading each other romantic poems, telling jokes.

He'd take her to his favorite beach, a secret cove of pink sand. It was on a beautiful island in the middle of a turquoise sea, and you could only reach it by boat. They'd swim and sun, and later they'd sail to the nearby whitewashed, red-roofed town, and anchor in the harbor. They'd have dinner at a private place he loved, with an outdoor terrace and a four-star sunset.

But each morning, the harsh, plain light of day rinsed his fantasies away. He might never find this girl, might never share anything with her again.

"You know, Will, there is one thing you haven't tried yet," Chris finally said, wiping a glob of catsup off his chin.

Will raised an eyebrow.

"Well, if you're so sure she lives around here, you could start knocking on doors. Maybe you'll have better luck."

Will shook his head immediately. "And if she isn't responding now because she doesn't want me to find her—"

"Then you don't have anything to lose," Kenny

said practically. "If I'd found someone so special, I wouldn't give up until I'd found her."

"Face it. You can't go out with a shoe forever," Chris added. "It could get a bit dull."

"Man, but I can't go around ringing every doorbell," Will said as a new realization hit him. "You think the press liked my little newspaper announcement, imagine what they'd do with me going door-to-door like a traveling salesman. A media circus. No way. My parents would find out, and I'd be home faster than you could say 'paparazzi'."

"Paparazzi. Before I met you, I always thought it was like some special kind of pizza," Kenny mused.

Will gave a short laugh. "I'd like to throw a pizza at those guys some of the time. Get that gooey, sticky extra cheese all over the fancy cameras they stick in my face."

"Hey, are we talking pizza, or are we coming up with a plan?" Chris asked. "Okay, Will can't go around banging on doors. So I guess that means we'll have to do it. Right, Kenny? We'll take the shoe—don't worry, Will, we'll treat it with the utmost respect—and we'll start looking for the girl who owns its match. Discreetly. If anyone asks, you don't know anything about it. We're doing it all on our own."

Will felt a bubble of guarded optimism. "Well, it's something. And you guys would do that for me? You really wouldn't mind?"

"Anything for love," Kenny said, and then noisily slurped up the remains of his shake.

"Of course it's a big favor," Chris said. "You'll owe us big time, Will. I mean, imagine it. Poor us, meeting every pretty girl in town. . . ."

There it was again—her glass shoe! Two boys she'd never seen before were at the front door, talking to Lucinda and holding Ella's shoe! At first glance, she thought she might be seeing things. After all, it was the only thing she'd thought about since Lucinda showed her the newspaper article. The newspaper photo of her shoe inside the heart, her magical evening with the boy, her wonder at who he'd turned out to be . . . and how it could have happened at all. That and her inescapable, profound longing to see him again—to talk with him and feel him close to her—mingled with the heartbreaking understanding that she never would. She could never let him know who she really was.

Ella turned the vacuum cleaner off and edged closer to the door.

"So you see, we know how happy it would make Prince Will if we could find out anything about the young lady who wore this shoe to his party," Ella heard the large sweet-faced boy with the dark hair say to Lucinda. His friend, lean and classically handsome with blond, curly hair, held on to the shoe. No, Ella's eyes weren't playing tricks on her. The prince wanted to find her.

She felt a surge of happiness . . . and a crashing wave of gloom. Part of her wanted to run over to the boys, another part told her to run and hide. Ella took a step back into the living room, and peered out from around the doorjamb. The boys wouldn't spot her as easily now.

But Lucinda seemed to have a sense of exactly where Ella was. At that moment, she turned her head and her cold green-eyed gaze met Ella's. Ella was frozen by it. Lucinda turned back to the boys. "Well, both my daughters were guests at the prince's party," she said, her voice oozing fake sweetness.

"And does this belong to one of them?" the blond boy asked eagerly, holding out the glass shoe.

Lucinda had to know that Staci's long, thin canoe of a foot would never fit into that shoe. She'd have to chop off her big toe. Nor would Drew's fat, stubby tugboat foot.

Ella stood motionless as Lucinda held out her

hand. "Well, it looks familiar. Let me take a closer look."

The blond boy gave her the shoe.

Ella's body went tight. *No!* she wanted to yell. And then, in an awful scene she'd witnessed once before, the shoe just happened to slip from Lucinda's bony hand. It crashed against the shiny, black-and-white tile floor. In a terrible *déjà vu*, Ella saw it lying there in numerous jagged pieces.

Ella bit her lip to keep from crying out as she watched the two boys scramble to pick up pieces of the broken shoe. Ella saw a mean blotch of red bloom on the lean one's finger.

"Oh, I'm so terribly sorry," Lucinda said falsely.

The boys were shaking their heads as they collected all the pieces of Ella's shoe and hurried off. Lucinda shut the door after them. The smile dropped off her face.

As she passed Ella, she spoke without even glancing at her. "You'd better clean up over there."

Ella looked at the floor by the doorway and saw the last trace of her wonderful evening: an ugly streak of red on the black-and-white tiles.

She couldn't expect the magic to last forever, could she?

Fifteen

Will stared at the pieces of glass and at Chris's bandage-swaddled finger. "You broke the shoe." He felt a rising panic. That shoe—it was his only link to his true love—whoever and wherever she was.

"Will, we're really sorry. It wasn't our fault. You gotta believe us," Chris began, still standing in the doorway.

"This lady—she was telling us about her two daughters," Kenny picked up. "She thought the shoe looked familiar. She wanted a closer look at it, and it just sort of slipped out of her hand—"

"Wait a sec! The shoe looked familiar?" Suddenly the fact that it was broken didn't matter as much to Will. He felt a rush of hope. "She'd seen it before?"

"Well, maybe she had," Chris explained. "You going to let us in?"

"Oh, yeah, sure, sorry." Will said distractedly, stepping aside to let his friends into his room. "And so you met the daughters? Was one of them . . . her? The girl I'm looking for?" He felt his blood racing.

Chris and Kenny exchanged looks. "Well, after the shoe got broken . . . See, we didn't get a chance. I mean, we haven't met the daughters yet."

"What?" Will was outraged. "The girl of my dreams might have been right under the same roof with you, and you didn't find out?"

Chris settled on the edge of Will's bed. "Calm down, man. You have to understand that at half the houses we went to, people claimed the shoe was theirs or their daughter's. Claimed they'd lost the other one, couldn't find it, or they'd thrown it out because they no longer had a pair. This one lady—she had to be getting up there in years—insisted on trying to squash her big, fat foot right into it. I'm surprised it didn't bust right then and there. Plus, my finger was bleeding like crazy. I just came from having it stitched up. Three big ones, okay? So we're sorry if we didn't stick around, gushing blood on that lady's floor."

"And anyway," Kenny added, flopping his weight into Will's armchair, "I didn't see any blue car parked at that house. Got a peek in the garage, too. A red Beamer—real nice, and a silver VW. Oh, and a blue bike parked outside the house, but no sports car like the one you'd described."

Carefully, Will collected the pieces of the shoe from Chris and gently put them on his desk. "So you mean you didn't have any luck at all?" He felt the stirrings of desperation.

"Got a few phone numbers—some pretty girls," Chris said. "And this bum finger, too."

"Stop being such a loser, man," Kenny chided him. "No, we didn't pick up any real clues. But we've got loads and loads more houses to go to. Of course, without the shoe—"

Will shook his head. "Forget it. I guess it really doesn't matter, does it? I don't need a shoe to recognize the girl I'm looking for. I'd know her in a second. It just means I'm going to have to go along with you guys."

"But what about when the word gets around?" Kenny asked. "When those pappa-whatchamacallits find out?"

Will squared his shoulders. "I'll figure something out. Or maybe I won't. But I can't sit here and do nothing anymore. Not when she might be so nearby. We'll start where you left off, blue car or no." He pulled his parka out of the closet. "What are we waiting for?"

*   *   *

This was the meaning of agony. Ella sat in the dining room, a pile of mending in front of her, a darning needle and thread in her hand. The dining room doors were closed—Lucinda had made a point of shutting her in—but the voices in the foyer echoed loud and clear in the largely unfurnished space.

Ella could hear every word that was said—and every rise and fall in her prince's voice. He was right on the other side of the wall. The boy who'd danced so beautifully under the stars, who'd known the names of so many constellations, who had been smart and handsome and had told her she was special. All she had to do was open the door between them, and she'd see him again. It was that simple. And that out of the question.

Ella couldn't rid herself of the sting of Lucinda's earlier words. "He'll be delighted to hear how beautifully you wash and iron." Ella could imagine the look of shock on the prince's handsome face if he found her sitting here, darning her stepsisters' sweaters. Well, there was no way he was going to find out about her. No. Let him remember their one evening together with longing.

"Well, it's very nice to see you again, Drew, and to meet your mother and sister," Ella heard Prince William say. Oh, his rich, full voice. The one that had called after her to stay with him. Ella fought back her tears. Where was the magic now? "But I'm afraid we can't spend any more time here," she heard him continue. "We have many more houses to try."

Oh, please don't go! Ella wanted to call out. *Let me look at you one more time. Not in a picture, with the title Prince William printed underneath, but face to face, spirit to spirit, two nobodies for just another moment.* She felt the weight of the glass shoe straining the seams of her old sweatshirt pocket.

"But why go on a wild-goose chase in the cold?" Ella heard Lucinda say in a syrupy voice. "You and Drew should take the chance to get to know each other better. And, Staci, you can entertain the prince's charming young friends."

"No, that's not possible," a different voice said quickly—one of the friends, no doubt.

"But thank you for your time," Ella heard the prince say politely. "Good afternoon."

Ella could taste the tears at the back of her throat. "Good-bye, Prince William," she whispered. And without warning, she found herself bursting into sobs. She dropped her head into her hands to muffle the noise, but her breaths came wet and loud and full of misery.

"What was that?" she heard the prince asking through the closed door.

"What was what?" Drew's voice. Or maybe Staci's.

"Crying. Someone's crying. Who's back there?" Prince William asked.

Ella swallowed her sobs.

"That's . . . nobody," Lucinda returned.

"Nobody?" he asked. *Two nobodies.* "Nobody—that's exactly who I'm looking for!"

Ella's heart pounded out a wild drumroll.

"But, ah—it's just our—our maid, Ella," Lucinda stammered.

"With your permission, ma'am . . ." Ella heard Prince William's voice getting closer.

She couldn't resist the chance to see him again. She couldn't let him just walk away from her. But she also couldn't let him find out she wasn't who he thought she was. She was torn in two directions.

But before she had time to decide what to do, the dining-room door was opened. She looked up with moist eyes. Her breath caught. Their gazes locked.

And then she saw it. The look of shock she'd been most afraid of seeing on his fine-boned face. It was all she could do to keep from sobbing again.

"It's you!" he whispered incredulously.

Ella fought the fresh onslaught of tears. Swallowing them back, she reached into her pocket with a trembling hand and pulled out her shoe. She held it toward him. "I'm sorry," she cried.

He reached for the shoe, and their hands touched. Ella felt a warm tingle. *Oh, Prince William.*

He didn't pull away. "Sorry? Why?" He sounded genuinely puzzled. "Ella." Ella thrilled to the sound of her name on his lips, the touch of their fingers. "What a beautiful name," he said. "I'm Will, and I'm so happy I found you. But—" he took his hand away, and the shoe with it "—why didn't you want to be found?"

"I didn't want you to see that I really *am* a nobody. I didn't mean to fool you. The car, the fancy clothes—they . . . weren't really mine."

Will shook his head. "You're no more a nobody than I am. Than anyone else is. How can you think that? I don't care if you're rich or poor or what you have or don't. I don't care who you are on the surface. Maybe you'll think it's silly of me—" he sounded a bit shy "—but I feel as if I got to know who you really are—deep inside. Even though we had so little time together."

Ella nodded. "I felt that way, too." But she

didn't dare give in to the spark of hope that was ready to burst out of her heart.

"I want to talk to you again, to look at the stars with you again."

"You do? Oh, so do I," Ella said.

"That foundation you were talking about—the one for people in need? Well, who's going to help me set it up? It was your idea. Please. Don't run from me anymore. Please, Ella."

He can't really mean it. Does he really want to be with me? And then the prince knelt down before her. A prince! *Her* prince, knelt down in front of her, Ella, and her pile of mending! "May I put this shoe on you?" he asked, holding out her glass shoe.

Ella felt a giggle rising in her throat. She couldn't hold it in. And then Will was giggling, too, as he unlaced her thin, old sneaker and took it off, then slipped the glass shoe over her sock.

Ella felt a funny tingle—a peppermint tingle like the night of the party. And for a split second, she was clothed in velvet and mirrors just as she'd been that magical night. Numerous gasps reminded her that she and Will had an audience.

Ella felt a shadow of self-consciousness. There were the two boys she'd seen on her doorstep earlier, a big white bandage on the blond one's finger.

Both boys looked absolutely stunned. And Lucinda even more so. And then, in the blink of an eye, the pretty clothes vanished again, and Ella was once more in her jeans and old sweatshirt, the glass shoe on over her sock.

"Whoa," Will said softly, "for a second, I thought . . ." He shook his head. "Well, never mind. I guess that's how I'll always think of you." Then he stood up and took Ella's hands, helping her out of her chair. Their eyes searched one another, and Ella remembered how wonderful it was to talk to him, and how easily and naturally they'd danced together. Perhaps they really did understand each other, and maybe they weren't as different as she feared.

"There must be some mistake," Ella heard Lucinda mutter. Ella had a terrifying moment. Could Lucinda be right?

But Will shook his head without ever taking his eyes off Ella. "No mistake. That was a special night we shared," he said quietly, "but I don't want it to be our last. I want it to be the first of many. Of a lifetime, Ella . . ."

"Oh, me, too, Will. Me, too." Ella was in her prince's arms, and she didn't care who was watching.

Sixteen

"Miss, miss. Over here" called out a reporter with a pad and paper.

A huge mob of photographers began snapping pictures the moment Ella and Will stepped out of her house. Will had told her to expect a crowd, but this was crazy. How did so many people find out about their private plans?

"Ella, some people are saying you're like a young Grace Kelly—the 1950s movie star who became a princess. What do you think? Are you the next Grace Kelly?"

Ella smiled graciously, which wasn't a hard thing for her to do. She was bursting with happiness. "I think she was great in *Rear Window*."

"And will you be a princess, like she was?"

"Well, there aren't any plans yet," Ella answered. But she had a marvelous feeling—yes, a magical feeling—that she really was going to live happily ever after.

She and Will made their way toward the waiting limo, the driver following behind them with Ella's luggage. Soon they'd be heading for the coast, to the harbor where the royal yacht was waiting to set sail. Christmas in the palace! Ella couldn't have imagined it in her wildest dreams when she was scrubbing and vacuuming and falling in tearful exhaustion onto her little attic mattress.

Oh, Fay, I wish I knew where you were. I need to thank you for all you've done for me, Ella thought. *Thank, you, thank you, if you can hear me wherever you are.*

Ella took a last look back at the house—at Lucinda's house. Suddenly, in the middle of so much joy, she felt a tiny tug of sadness. Once upon a time this house had been hers and her father's and mother's. Once upon a time she had learned to ride a two-wheeler in the driveway, Dad running behind her to steady her by the back of the seat. She had celebrated birthdays in the yard, grown up under this roof.

"You okay?" Will leaned down to whisper to her.

Ella patted the star-shaped cookie cutter in her pocket. It was the one she'd remembered using with Mom, to make their Christmas sugar cookies. Ella had slipped it off the pegboard on her way out of the house. "Yeah, I'm okay," she told Will. She had her memories. But that part of her life was over. It was time to look ahead.

Ella let her eyes wander over the crowd until she spotted Steph trying to squeeze her way through the throng of people. "Oh, I need to say good-bye to Steph."

"No problem. Chris and Kenny are supposedly around here someplace." Will glanced about. "Hey, there they are. Why don't you take a few minutes alone with your friend, then come over and introduce her."

Ella nodded. Will had to be the most considerate, the most handsome, the best kisser . . . She felt herself blushing as she made her way toward Steph, the photographers recording her every step.

She pulled Steph aside, away from the crowd. "Oh, Ella, I'm so happy for you," Steph said.

"Me, too."

"He's so handsome."

Ella grinned. "He's wonderful, too. Oh, Steph, it's all so amazing!" Impulsively, she threw her arms around Steph.

Steph gave her a bear hug back. "Hey, Ella?" she said seriously, as they released each other.

"Listen, I've missed you lately. Really missed you. And I'm happy for you and all, but I'm going to miss you even worse now."

Ella nodded. "Yeah, same here. I'm going to miss you, too."

Steph rummaged around in the knapsack slung over her shoulder. "I have a little bon-voyage present for you." She pulled out a silver package, the size of a CD box. "In case you get homesick for some American rock and roll," she said, handing Ella the gift.

Ella tore off the shiny paper. "Oh, cool. Red Stripe Unplugged. They're my favorite band." Ella realized that with all the excitement before her trip, she hadn't gotten Steph a thing in return. In a wave of good feeling, she felt around under her coat sleeve and unclasped her charm bracelet. "Here. I know you always liked this."

Steph shook her head. "Ella, I can't. I mean, you've had that since second grade. It's like your trademark or something.

Ella shrugged. "Just until I see you again, okay? To remember me. Besides, I've had plenty of other lucky charms lately. And I don't mean the silver kind."

Steph smiled. "You mean it? Oh, wow! I'll take really good care of it—and I'll wear it every day. I promise." She let Ella help her fasten it. "So when *will* we see each other again?"

Ella gave a little sigh. "Well, actually, I don't know."

"You mean, there's no plan?"

"Sort of. I'm going to be Will's date for all his Christmas parties. Get a chance to meet people, see what it's like to be part of all the palace events." Ella got a case of butterflies in her stomach at just the thought of it all. "Then—who knows? The king and queen told Will they were getting excellent publicity on the foundation I helped him set up."

"Yeah," Steph said, "it was so cool to read about you in the newspaper. I was so proud. And Jane and I are thinking about volunteering there after school. We'd like to help out too."

"Oh, Steph, that's so great."

Steph nodded. "So, Will's parents are psyched, too. That's cool. The royal seal of approval, huh?"

Ella laughed. "Yeah, it's kind of strange. They think I'm a good influence on Will, or something. I'm just happy, and I want to spread it around. Anyway, I only hope it goes as well when I meet them in person. Will's already asked if they think I'm a good enough influence to take under their wing. You know, become like a ward of the palace and finish school there. Until Will finishes up at Chason and we're ready to get married."

Steph let out a squeal of excitement. "Oh, wow, Ella. Married! To the prince!"

Ella grinned. She felt light-headed and happy.

"And you'd be the princess?" Steph went on.

"I know—it's impossible to believe. I can't accept all this yet. Everything's happening so fast."

Then Steph's smile drooped. "But that means you might not come back here at all. Ella, I don't know whether to be sorry for me or happy for you. Both, I guess."

"Well, don't go calling me 'Mrs.' yet. Or 'Mrs. Highness'." Ella giggled. "I mean, I'm not exactly from the right kind of family to marry a prince. Ha. Can you imagine Lucinda and company as royals? In their own minds, maybe, but that's about the extent of it."

Steph nodded. "Well, what does Will say about that?"

Ella glanced over at Will. He and Chris and Kenny were laughing away. Ella felt as if she could burst with love. "He says that if his parents don't give us their approval to get engaged, he's going to do it anyway. That he'll even give up his claim to the throne, if he has to."

Steph's brown eyes opened wide. "Oh, wow!

He said that? He'd do that for you? Ella, that's so incredible. But wait! Then you won't be a princess."

Ella nodded. "Yeah. But that would be okay. Really. I mean, I knew I was in love with Will before I had any idea who he was." Ella couldn't hold back a gooey kind of sigh. "But anyway, hopefully he won't have to give anything up," she added, keeping her voice too low for the ears of prying reporters. "His parents said it sounded as if he'd made up his mind already, and that was a good sign, because he was going to have lots of important decisions to make as king. And that changing some of the outdated customs was what a country needed in a king to lead them into the next century."

"A king!" Steph said, shaking her head in amazement. "Listen to you. You're talking about your own boyfriend!"

Ella grabbed Steph's hand. "My boyfriend. You know, right now that's as awesome as anything else. Palaces, royals, birthrights are one thing . . . but Will's my boyfriend, and I'm just so happy."

"Well, I'll miss you," Steph said.

"Me, too. I'll miss you, too. Write, me, okay? Keep me posted on what's happening at home."

"I will. Hey, Lucinda and your stepmonsters didn't even come outside to see you off."

Ella colored with embarrassment. "Actually, I lied to them about when I was leaving. Maybe it was awful of me. I picked a time when I knew they wouldn't be around. I just didn't want to have them be any part of what's ahead for me." Ella sighed. "I suppose I could have been nicer to them, but it's too late now."

Steph raised her shoulders. "Why? They were never even the tiniest bit generous with you. Totally the opposite."

"Yeah, although ever since Will came along, you wouldn't believe how fake-sweet they've been. 'Oh, Ella, let us do those dishes. Come shopping with us, Ella. You deserve some new clothes.' They're such hypocrites. At least when they were witches, they were being themselves, you know? I can just hear the fights they're going to have when they get home—whose fault it was that they let a prince walk away from here, who was meaner to me, who's going to do the house chores now. Actually, they've already started on that one." Ella smiled. "I feel sorry for them. There just isn't the smallest amount of happiness in any of them."

Steph gave a hard laugh. "Ella, they deserve each other."

Ella shrugged. "Maybe it's the best revenge. Still . . ."

"Oh, hey," Steph said, looking to the other edge of the crowd. "There are the prince's friends—the ones Jane and I saw at the flea market."

"Oh, yeah. Will said we should go over and say hi. You thought his friend Chris was pretty cute, didn't you?"

"The blond one? Jane really liked him. I thought he was a little high on himself, actually. I mean, I know he's Will's friend and all. . . . But the other one seemed nice. Kind of shy, though."

"Kenny? Yeah, he's a sweetheart. Come on. I'll give you the official introduction."

They all chatted for a few moments, doing their best to ignore the cameras. Suddenly a commotion spread through the crowd, as a red sports car came screeching up the driveway. Ella felt herself go tense. Lucinda and her obnoxious daughters.

Will's bodyguards came to attention. Lucinda slammed on her brakes in front of all the onlookers, and she and Staci and Drew stormed out of their car.

"Oh, Ella, thank goodness we didn't miss your bon voyage!" Lucinda exclaimed, flashing a toothpaste-commercial smile at the cameras. "So nice to see you again, Your Highness."

One of the bodyguards stepped forward—a bulky, dark-haired man with the build of a linebacker. "Is this someone you know, Your Majesty?"

Ella wished she and Will had snuck out of there just a few minutes sooner.

But Will simply shook his head. "She's . . . nobody," he said. "Just my fiancée's, ah, maid and her girls."

Ella recognized the exact words Lucinda had said to Will when he'd finally found her. She allowed herself an easy laugh as Lucinda, Staci, and Drew slunk away toward the house.

"Are you ready, Ella?" Will asked, holding out his hand to her.

Ella hugged Steph hard, then nodded at Will.

Will took her hand. She felt the warmth of their fingers intertwined as they got into the limo. "Hey, man," Will said out the window to Chris as the driver was buckling up. "Remember what we talked about."

And then they pulled away, the bodyguards in a car behind them, the gravel crunching under their tires. Ella settled into the soft, buttery leather seat cushions. There was a television in front of her, a telephone, and a full bar. Soft jazz was already coming from hidden rear speakers. She watched Will pour her a champagne glass of sparkling cider. "So, what were you and Chris talking about?" she asked.

Will laughed. "Oh, he said he thought I was

pretty brave to risk making a fool of myself over you—to risk having you turn me down in public and stuff."

Ella took her glass from Will and snuggled close to him. "You didn't risk anything,"

Will gave her a soft kiss on the cheek. "Yeah, well, I didn't know that at the time. And Chris— well, he's afraid to tell this girl how he feels. Like, suppose she doesn't want to go out with him?" Will took a sip of his cider. "He thinks it's easier not to put himself in a position to get hurt. So I told him if he doesn't risk anything, he won't get anything in return. He wouldn't go as far as saying it, but we both knew we were talking about him and this girl Trish. I told him not to waste any more time. To go talk to her right now. Tell her he really doesn't want any other girls."

Ella looked out of the smoked glass rear window. "Well, it looks like he took your advice. I don't see him out there anymore."

"Good. Hey, it looks like Kenny and your friend Steph have plenty to say to each other," Will remarked as the limo made a right turn out of the driveway.

Suddenly Ella saw a rusty van racing next to them. She immediately banged on the partition between her and the driver. The glass divider slid down smoothly. "Sir, could you please stop the car for just a moment?" she asked with urgency. "Right here. If you could pull up alongside that van that's coming in the other direction . . ." Ella pushed the button to lower her window and stuck her head out. "Fay! Fay!"

Fay's round face, framed by a fluff of white hair, leaned out of her van window. "Oh, my, I almost missed you, dear."

"Fay, I'm so glad to see you. I wanted to say good-bye to you. Will, this is my special friend Fay. I told you about her the other day. She's the one who inspired me to start thinking about the foundation. Oh, Fay, I wish I could find some way to—"

"You don't have to," Fay stopped her, before she could finish her sentence. "Your foundation— it's thanks many times over. Thanks to you and thanks to His Highness."

"We're just glad we could help," Will replied.

"You take care of yourself," Ella said.

"And you, my dear. Live happily ever after. It's not always easy, but I know you'll do it. An honor to meet you, Your Highness."

Will gave a little bow of his head.

"Now, run along, you two. I don't want you to miss the sunset from the deck of your boat," Fay said. "Good-bye, Ella."

"How did she know we planned it to set sail at sunset?" Will asked in astonishment, as the limo started moving again. "I thought you said you haven't seen her since the night we met."

Ella shook her head. "I haven't. Call it woman's intuition, I guess. Fay—well, she just knows things."

Out the limo window, the familiar houses of Ella's street rolled by and out of view. She might be leaving her old life forever. It was a bittersweet feeling. But there was so much to look forward to.

"Does she know how much I love you?" Will asked softly, taking both their glasses and placing them in a built-in holder. He reached for Ella and drew her close.

She gazed into his hazel eyes, and gently traced the line of his lips with the tips of her fingers. And then the past vanished in the depths of their kiss. His lips were sweet and moist. He cupped her face with strong, warm hands. Ella breathed in his nearness, every inch of her deliciously aware of him. They kissed again and again, holding each other tenderly but tightly.

Ella was about to sail off into the sunset with her prince. But it wasn't a fairy-tale ending. No, not an ending at all. It was the beginning of a perfect, beautiful life.

About the Author

Jennifer Baker is the author of two dozen young adult and middle grade novels, including Scholastic's *First Comes Love* quartet. She is also the producer for TV Guide's Online teen area and teaches creative writing workshops for elementary and junior high school students. She lives in New York City with her husband and son.